A HUNT IN MAGIC CITY

A HUNT IN MAGIC CITY

MAGIC CITY CHRONICLES™ BOOK FIVE

TR CAMERON   MICHAEL ANDERLE   MARTHA CARR

DISRUPTIVE IMAGINATION®

LMBPN Publishing
PMB 196, 2540 South Maryland Pkwy
Las Vegas, NV 89109

First Edition May, 2021
ebook ISBN: 978-1-64971-722-1
Print ISBN: 978-1-64971-723-8

THE A HUNT IN MAGIC CITY TEAM

Thanks to the JIT Readers

Dave Hicks
Wendy L Bonell
Diane L. Smith
Dorothy Lloyd
Larry Omans
John Ashmore
Angel LaVey
Paul Westman

If I've missed anyone, please let me know!

Editor
Skyhunter Editing Team

DEDICATION

For those who seek wonder around every corner and in each turning page. Thank you choosing to share the adventure with me. And, as always, for Dylan and Laurel.

— TR Cameron

CHAPTER ONE

Bad thoughts bounced around Ruby Achera's brain as she hurtled along the desert highway, seeking relief. *Highway, hell. Two lanes, imperfectly paved, twisting and turning at random is not my definition of a highway.* The motorcycle purred beneath her as she wound through the turns, barely enough of her intellectual capacity devoted to the process to keep her on the road. The rest of it battled the insidious mental messages the artifact in her left forearm pummeled her with. She'd won the initial battle and had presumed the ones to come would be less fierce, or at least less constant. Instead, every time her mind wandered, the Atlantean magic sought to increase its influence upon her.

Those murmurings had pushed her out of bed at two in the morning, sent her straight to the motorcycle and out onto the road. The full black helmet completely obscured her features, the anonymity giving her a sense of freedom. Her black leather uniform top hid the tattoo that was the external proof of the artifact's existence. On its own, the bottom layer of her costume was generic enough not to connect to her identity as Magic City's defender, and the tunic and trousers offered the best protection possible against any sort of damage short of a full suit of body armor. Her high boots laced halfway up her calves, and thin riding gloves covered her hands to protect them from the whipping sand.

She carried fewer weapons than usual because Ruby Achera, allegedly adopted scion of the family who owned Spirits casino on the Ely Strip, wouldn't have a good reason to lug them around. The artifact mocked her for all the identities she possessed, and she growled and accelerated. The ARCH 1 leapt underneath her like an eager horse and sped forward. Although as a Mist Elf she could always turn to her magic, she still hadn't been comfortable leaving all of her offensive tools behind. A document tube strapped diagonally across her back concealed her sword, as yet unnamed, and the pair of personalities it contained. She had turned to them more than once to help her fight off the artifact's influence, but even that had become more a chore than a relief.

This moment, flying along the highway in the dark, under the stars, alone in the middle of nowhere, was decidedly *not* a chore. It gave her a sense of liberation, something she hadn't felt too often since her return to Magic City. Out here, she could even portion off a part of her thoughts to consider the future, about the techno-magical items she might create, about where her relationship with Demetrius could go, about fulfilling her destiny on the other planet.

A low chuckle rumbled through her mind. *Indeed. Once*

you have amassed all that power, then I will take you as my own.

"Shut the hell up, you scummy bastard." She'd turned insulting the artifact into a stupid game that nonetheless amused her, and her names for it ranged from the most sophisticated insults to the basest epithets. She stiffened slightly as her phone vibrated in her pocket, but she didn't dare take her focus off the highway to see who sought her attention. *You definitely don't text and drive when you're on a motorcycle, not if you want to be alive at the end of the ride.*

A notice at the side of the road proclaimed Cherin, Nevada, a mile ahead. The sign was as dilapidated as the town it heralded, a remnant of a time left behind by the modern world. She'd been through the area several times before on rides similar to this one, though not with the artifact murmuring in her head and not quite so late at night. It was a crossroads with an old filling station, now shut down, a four-unit motel that had probably been dismal in its prime but was currently clearly vacant and boarded up, and what had been a diner, a squat building that had mostly fallen in upon itself. *That reminds me, we still need to clear that second escape tunnel from the bunker.* They'd discovered the passage ended beneath a collapsed building, and Margrave assured her it would be easy enough to build up a protective structure not visible from the outside to permit its use.

The voice in her head offered no comment on that particular plan, and she sighed in relief. She came around a bend and spotted the gas station ahead to her right, opposite the diner on her left. The once-motel held a position on the diagonal from the gas station across the intersection.

A glint caught her eye from a place where a glimmer shouldn't be, the roof of the squat building that serviced the fuel pumps. It preceded the sound by only an instant, the report of a rifle loud and echoing in the empty desert. *Guess there's no need for a silencer out here*, her brain supplied unhelpfully. The bike jerked and flipped, sending her hurtling through the air. *Front tire hit*, her mind offered, again with no particular benefit.

Her reflexive force shield, which had saved her when the bar at the Mist had exploded in her face to welcome her back to town, was already forming around her. She automatically calculated angles and trajectory, allowing the protective cocoon to solidify before using more force magic to cushion her landing and keep her from scraping her way across the road. Feedback from the impact and continued motion transmitted through the shield as a sensation similar to pain, but nothing like the real damage and agony the accident would've caused.

She wobbled up to her feet, shivering with adrenaline. The involuntary meeting with the ground had spider-webbed her faceplate, and she pulled off the helmet and dropped it to the pavement. She'd landed more or less in the middle of the intersection before sliding through it. Motion drew her eye to the three figures advancing toward her, one from the diner, one from the gas station, and one from the hotel. The third was the nearest, so she charged that one.

The figure was human, a woman, and raised a rifle in response to her rush. It spat bullets out at her in a stream, and Ruby slashed her hand across on a diagonal, creating an angled shield to intercept and deflect them. *No way they've got anti-magic rounds. If they were that competent, they wouldn't have missed me and hit the bike in the first place.* She didn't make the mistake of assuming they were amateurs. Probably, they were pretty good at what they did, but no one would send their most expensive team against Ruby Achera. There would be no reason since as far as the world knew, she was the dilettante adopted human daughter of wealthy parents. *Entrepreneur. Innovator.* The words she'd used with her family in jest filtered through her mind randomly.

Ruby snarled, "Okay, wench, innovate this." At a distance of ten feet, she sent a large force wave at the other woman, throwing her backward toward the motel. Ruby continued running, feeling the presence of the rest of the enemy team. If she stopped, they'd be in range in an instant. As it was, handgun rounds *splatted* near her, but none connected. Even if they had, her personal shield, which lay a couple of inches away from her skin, would have dealt with them handily. *As long as they aren't super heavy caliber, that is.* The things she'd read suggested that a big enough bullet could deliver sufficient kinetic energy even through a shield to take her out of the fight, and without anyone around to help, that would likely be fatal.

The woman pushed herself to her feet with her back pressed against a plywood panel covering the entrance to one of the middle units for support. Ruby strengthened her shield, pumped some magic into her muscles to increase her speed and strength, and slammed into her foe, leading with her shoulder.

In the instant before impact, her opponent's eyes widened, and she tried to bring the rifle up toward Ruby's face. It got caught between their bodies as the collision blasted the woman back through the plywood, sending both of them tumbling into the room. Dust and the scent of sour mold filled her senses, and she gagged before launching another force wave outward to clear the air of nearby particles. The plaster in the ceiling cracked, the walls creaked, and moving things on the floor scuttled further away. The woman under her groaned weakly, and Ruby lifted far enough to whip an elbow into the woman's head, knocking her out at a minimum. It wasn't time for niceties, not with at least two more on the way. *And probably a third, given the rifle shot.*

A four-member team made sense. *Guess the only question is whether the rifle person will stay on watch in case I try to escape. Fifty-fifty chance.* The others were doubtless approaching the motel at that very second, hopefully with enough caution to slow them a little. Ruby called up a small ball of light in her left hand and used it to examine the woman, finding what she was looking for after only a couple of moments. The radio was a military knockoff often adopted by private security. *Also by, whoever these guys are. Wonder if they're from Aces. I wouldn't be surprised if those bastards were behind this. Still, why would* they *care about Ruby Achera?*

Those thoughts cascaded through her mind unproductively as she liberated the radio and tucked the earpiece into her ear. No sound was present at the moment, which she attributed to good discipline. If she'd been dealing with amateurs, she would've expected conversation. Professionals only talked when they needed to. She checked the room, staying low and extending the light around, and discovered connecting doors to both sides. A window looked out onto an expanse of dirt and scrub in the back, and the notion of slipping under a veil and escaping was immediately appealing.

She wasn't going to do that for a bunch of reasons. First, she wanted to know why these people had targeted her in particular. Second, she needed to know how they'd found her riding in the desert in the middle of the night. Third, and perhaps most importantly, she had to see if they had any link to Aces Security or any of the other logical connections in town that Gabriel Sloane might've contracted before his death. *Because if he left instructions behind when he shuffled off to the afterlife, that could be bad.* Really *bad.*

She stood and moved toward the connecting door that led to the next unit over, the other occupying the center of the building. *Fourth, you scumbags wrecked my beautiful bike. Somebody's going to pay for that.*

CHAPTER TWO

The room on the opposite side of the door was as wrecked as the one she'd left. A small nightstand was disintegrating beside a bed with a half-broken frame. This chamber looked like it might have hosted a party at some point, to judge by the beer cans scattered around.

The open door threw moonlight into the space, illuminating the most important feature of the room. A man dressed in the same black fatigues as the woman she'd defeated, raising an identical rifle. Ruby said, "No, I don't think so." The statement held no warmth or amusement. Fury battered at her mental defenses with the taste of the artifact's influence underlying it. She reached out with her force magic and grabbed the weapon, yanking her arm back to hurl it across the chamber. The man slapped the release catch so he didn't go with it, unfortunately, and drew the pair of pistols holstered at his thighs.

Ruby shook her head. "I said, *no.*" She thrust out her palms and blasted each weapon with a bolt of force, knocking them away. "Here's the deal, scumbag. You and your friends have made a huge bloody mistake. Now you're going to tell me everything you know about what brought you here and how you found me, or I'll break each bone in your body until you do. Starting with these." She reached out her hand and squeezed, imagining a fist gathering around his fingers, curling them inward. His bones snapped with a series of audible pops. Dark elation surged inside her, and she pushed it away with a growl. *I'm in charge, you bastard.* The Atlantean's laughter rippled in her skull.

She strode forward unhurriedly, and he backed toward the room's exit, cradling his crushed appendage. A sharp gesture summoned a wall of force to block the doorway he'd entered through and continued her advance. He growled something obscene and drew a knife with his functional hand. Ruby shook her head again. "Okay, you don't seem to get it. So, take your shot." She spread her arms wide, and he darted in and stabbed the blade at her chest.

Her left arm whipped around in a block, intercepting the point and causing it to scrape on her shield as she pushed it harmlessly away. *I cut that one a little too close. Sure, it's unlikely he'd have an anti-magic weapon, but it was still a dumbass move.* She circled her right hand underneath and grabbed his wrist, then gave it a subtle twist and yanked to pull him forward. His shins banged off the bed, and he went down, the remaining structure collapsing beneath him and puffing out another cloud of dust and who knew what else.

She pushed the particles away from herself with magic while he coughed and gagged. When he'd recovered enough to roll over and glare at her, she said, "Want to live? Tell me something about what brought you here."

His voice was harsh, raspy, almost inaudible despite his effort to push words out of his throat. "Wrong information, apparently. We were targeting a human." He broke into a wave of coughing. *Well, I can't let you report back now. I bet Diana and her team have somewhere you can cool your heels for a while.*

The earpiece crackled with the words "Delta, Delta, Delta," and the man's eyes widened. His body lurched reflexively toward the door, and she instantly realized that whatever the code meant, he didn't want to be in the motel when it happened. Therefore, neither did she. She raced for the doorway, summoning an additional shield over the one that coated her body. A whistling sound signaled the arrival of something that slammed into and through the plywood covering the window.

The room behind her exploded, sending her hurtling forward in a tumble. The initial sound repeated as another munition landed, and the noise of the motel collapsing in on itself joined. *Not much loyalty from your comrades.* She rolled to her feet and located the gas station building, calling up a double-strength shield facing in that direction and dashing in a diagonal to the right away from it. *Where's contestant number three? Come out, come out, wherever you are.*

The sniper reaffirmed their presence as a bullet slammed into her shield at head level. *Thank heaven they didn't bring anti-magic. Probably trusting the element of surprise and the fact that their target wasn't a magical. Heh. For once, my parents' decision to hide my identity pays off.* She spotted the team's third member and shifted her path toward the man, who was pulling the trigger on a grenade launcher of some kind, to judge by the canister shooting from the barrel at high speed.

She'd never seen a weapon like it before. Her first thought was that maybe it shot rockets instead of grenades, but she knew exactly how to deal with it either way. She swung her hand in a slap toward the motel, and the projectile veered off in that direction. It hit and exploded, adding to the conflagration. She drew too close for him to use that weapon again, so he went for the pistol at his hip. It looked larger than usual, so she expended more energy to toughen up her shields. The sniper's bullet that struck the barrier guarding the back of her head had ample force to pitch her forward, and the round from the pistol smashed into her shin hard enough to send her tumbling. Her shields were great at protecting against penetration and at generally dissipating impacts, but those two rounds in quick succession hit it hard.

Ruby somersaulted and returned to her feet to find her quarry running away. "Oh no, you don't," she growled and reached for her power to throw out a line. Instead of her dominant right arm moving forward, her left arm did. The tattoo burned, and she guessed what was about to happen. A line of shadow magic reached out and wrapped itself around his feet. She reflexively yanked backward to drop him on his face, then slowed to a walk as she turned her attention inward. *You're not the boss of me.*

She pictured the Atlantean as his familiar laugh rang in her head. ***Is that so? Perhaps not yet. But soon. Very soon.***

Her foe in the real world stood, and Ruby punched him in the face, reinforcing the blow with force magic. He went down again, unconscious. She grabbed him by the collar and started dragging him toward the back of the motel, looking for some place to get him out of the way so she could deal with the last member of the team. The long gun barked, and the figure in her hand jerked. She looked down to see that the sniper had killed him, a clean shot to the heart that was spilling blood all over his chest. She dropped the body with a sigh and a curse. "Okay, scumbag. Let's do this."

She spared a portion of her magic to call up a veil, then let every shield other than the one running along her skin drop. Her abilities only allowed her to keep so many spells going at once, and the next would require some power. She ran to the back of the motel, then launched herself up and over it at the midpoint, flying through the air toward the sniper's likely position. From above, she got a clear view of a figure in black fatigues striding along the edge of the gas station roof with a rifle pointed at the motel, slowly panning the scope to spot her emergence.

It was doubtful the sniper would wait for long, but Ruby didn't need that much time. Before she hit the ground, she launched herself again, the distance requiring a second burst of force magic to get her there. She landed on the dusty surface behind the figure, who spun at the noise, whipping out a pistol. The sniper fired it automatically, almost without looking. The rounds smacked into Ruby's chest and stomach but didn't penetrate, thanks to her magic. She let the veil fall and simultaneously blasted the weapon away from the sniper, who turned out to be female. The other woman tried to wrench the heavy rifle around, and Ruby grabbed it with her force magic and yanked it aside to clatter on the roof.

The resolve in her foe's eyes was clear, and Ruby shook her head. "Nope." She whipped out a line of force from her right arm, carefully ensuring the artifact didn't influence her choice again and pulled the woman back from the edge she was about to throw herself over. "You would've barely gotten injured, much less killed. If there's going to be pain involved, I'd far prefer to be the one to supply it." She wrapped more force magic around her captive to keep her contained, reached down, and ripped out her earpiece. The woman struggled, cursed, and threatened, but Ruby paid no attention. She walked far enough away to be out of earshot and dialed a number on her phone, noting absently that the earlier alert had been a text from him.

Demetrius answered, "Hey Ruby, what's up? Awful late for you to be awake and not here."

The flirting drew a grin, even in the present circumstance. She replied, "Yeah, believe me, I'd much rather be there. Got some trouble. I need you to contact our government friends and tell them I have someone I'd like them to keep an eye on for me."

"I'll do it right now. Hold on."

Ruby walked over to the woman. "Don't fret. You'll probably live through this experience. Still, I can't have you reporting back to whoever sent you, so I'm afraid you're going to take a little vacation. I'm sure the facilities are nice."

Demetrius came back on the line. "I gave them your location. They'll open a portal to you soon."

"Excellent. Listen, someone came after me, and I'm not

sure how they found me. It's possible it was my bike since there probably aren't too many ARCH 1s around here, but I don't feel like I've ridden it in public. My bigger concern is that they might have tracked me from the house. Make sure all the defenses are okay."

"Wait one." He was gone for fifteen seconds, then reported, "Nothing to see here. No problems."

Ruby breathed a sigh of relief. "Great. Perfect. Listen, do a full diagnostic or whatever you do to verify nobody messed with stuff, and lock all the doors. Then, order me a bunch more drones. As soon as I have a free moment, I'll increase the house's surveillance and defense capability."

"Should I be worried?"

"I don't think so. You *should* be smart. You know, if you can stretch yourself to reach that lofty goal."

He coughed out the word "Loser" under his breath. "Hah. You owe me. I expect a real date for all the ongoing nonsense you put me through."

He broke through the worries that crowded her mind. She laughed. "You got it. I know just the place. As soon as I get a few things under control, we'll do it up big."

CHAPTER THREE

Julianna Sloane finished touching up her mascara and rose from the ivory and gold vanity in her dressing area. In the time since her husband's death, she'd progressed through the stages of grief quickly but intensely. *If I have a memoir one day, that would probably be a good title.* Her life had always been fast and furious, and she usually came out the other side victorious. *As I intend to do on this occasion as well.* She smoothed the jacket that matched her grey pinstripe pants, the low black heels underneath a perfect complementary shade. Her red blouse was the only splash of color, and she felt it was appropriate given the vengeance taken at her orders the night before.

She walked down the small hallway that led to the living room, which she'd altered since her husband's death. The white furniture was out, replaced by black versions that were more modern and less luxurious. *More me.* Still, it felt strange being there without him. For all that people saw her as a trophy wife, theirs had been a true partnership filled with real love.

She shrugged inwardly. *Now I'm on my own again. Certainly not a situation I'm a stranger to.* Julianna gave the man in the living room a thin smile. "Smith, good to see you." He had taken his usual pride in his appearance, his flattop perfectly even, the suit well-pressed. "Any changes to the schedule?"

His tones were lower and more respectful than they'd been toward her when she was only The Nightmare's wife. "No. All is as expected. Thompson is on her way up."

That brought a genuine smile to Julianna's lips. The newest member of her security's leadership was someone she'd long favored, but her husband hadn't been as gender-neutral as she was. *Or maybe he simply didn't recognize her talents. In any case, I do.* She was the alternate version of Smith—one or the other of them was with her during most of her waking time, or at least on call if she was somewhere safe, like the penthouse.

Julianna sat on the couch, and room service immediately bustled in. The uniformed waiter set a silver coffeepot and three heavy mugs on the table, along with a dish filled with a variety of cookies and berries. She nibbled on one of the latter while Smith poured coffee for the three of them.

Her newest lieutenant strode in, dressed in the standard security uniform of dark suit and black mock turtleneck. Her shoes were utilitarian but had a professional shine. A tight ponytail corralled her hair, giving her a sleek, no-nonsense look. Both the locks and her skin were a deep chestnut. Julianna said, "Good morning."

"How you doin', boss?" The other woman's informality

was one of the most appealing things about her. "Ready for the news?"

"Let me have it."

"Five out of the eight teams we sent were able to act on their targets. Results are one killed and three wounded. One escaped since we received the initial notification of contact but nothing from the team after."

Julianna frowned. "Who did we kill?"

"The eldest of the Caruthers."

"That's a pretty big family, multigenerational if I remember right. No immediate change will occur as a result. Who escaped?"

Thompson had the information ready, no need to unclasp her hands from behind her back to go for a device to look it up. "The Mist Elf family that's still in town. Achera. Eldest daughter."

"The human?" Julianna had gone over all the dossiers beforehand and had familiarized herself with the potential targets.

Her security both nodded. Smith interjected, "Yeah, her. The adopted one. Should have been easy, but apparently not."

Julianna shook her head. "Fifty percent success isn't a level I'm satisfied with. We need to do better. Include the surviving teams in the next set of operations since a shot at redemption might help motivate them. What did we learn from this experiment?"

Thompson replied, "The targets generally have good protection. Probably they increased it after Goryo did his thing." A nod urged her to continue. "We can guess they'll look for more security after last night, which will make the next phase somewhat more challenging."

Julianna waved her hand airily. "Part of the plan, all part of the plan. So. Smith, introduce Thompson to our security company principals. They are to start aggressively moving to absorb or eliminate their competition. When the casino owners in Ely contract new security, I want to be sure our people are part of whoever they choose. If it turns out they're not up to it, make a deal with a different company and offer them up as a sacrifice. Either way, we need to be on the inside when the ball gets rolling."

Smith replied, "Will do." He sounded eager to cause trouble for the two locals.

"Good. What else did we learn?"

Thompson replied, "Striking from a distance was effective in all four cases. Twice the snipers were adequate on their own, hitting the target with their first shot. In the other cases, the initial bullet was enough to give the team the opportunity to move in and do some damage before the defenders rallied. It's possible they'll be on guard against the snipers now, too. Certainly we should expect them to have more than one or two security guards with them."

Julianna shrugged and sipped her coffee, which was dark, rich, and bitter. She winced and dropped a single cube of sugar into it, poking at it with a long fingernail until it dissolved. Then she replied, "So change it up. I trust you to figure it out. What's essential is that when an opportunity presents itself, we're ready to hit it like a bolt of lightning from a cloudless sky. The more we thin out those families, the more likely they'll sell or get out of town.

Speaking of which, what's the situation inside the casinos themselves?"

Smith replied, "We've had teams visiting each of them every day. Heavily increased security, looks like some new detection equipment at the entrances. Both magicals and humans in uniform keeping an eye on things. Doubtless they have a bunch in plainclothes as well. It's unlikely we'll be able to get in undetected."

Julianna laughed. "That's probably what the pointy ears who owned the Mist thought, too. Right up until the moment it crashed down like a poorly stacked house of cards. I heard they ran back to their planet."

Thompson confirmed it. "Yep. The property is now in the hands of a trust. Our lawyers are working to see if there's a way to get at it, but it looks as if the documents were all written specifically to preclude an outside interest."

"Good choice on the family's part, anyway. They probably figured I'd have them killed to acquire the land, and they certainly weren't wrong." She took another drink of her coffee and ate a cookie, thinking. No other matters of import leapt to mind. "Thompson, get things started on setting up the next round of operations. Smith will be down presently so you can visit with our security company." She departed, and Julianna stood and wandered the living room. "Feels weird, here, without him." She looked out at the mountains in the distance. Before, they had comforted her. Now they were irrelevant. *Like most things.*

From behind her, her lieutenant replied, "Yeah. We were both with the boss for a long time. It's bound to take a while for things to seem like they're yours, instead of his."

An idea flashed through her brain with the abrupt power of an electrical charge. She turned and said, "You know what? You're exactly right. Inside and outside, everything here reminds me of him. It's time for a change if we want to leave that feeling behind. This apartment, hell, the whole town, has too many memories." Excitement at the idea coursed through her. "When you finish with the security company, find us a place in Vegas. Something high up, with a view of the Strip." She smiled with something approaching real happiness for the first time since her husband's death. "Yeah. A move to Sin City will be just the medicine I need."

CHAPTER FOUR

Ruby spun and slashed, leading with the artifact blade in her right hand and twisting to stab forward with the training blade in her left. Her imaginary opponent folded over the weapon as it pierced his stomach, then fell away. Ruby was already in motion toward the next, sweeping her lead sword up in a rising block and whipping the other low as she lifted her boot to intercept an imaginary kick.

It was still dark in her Oriceran village, with the sun barely peeking over the horizon. She'd been training for almost an hour, lost in practice, honing her skills and giving her mind a chance to rest. The only one of the people who'd attacked her and survived was now safely secured at Diana Sheen's base, and the agent had promised they would get whatever information was available from the captive. Ruby was still too keyed up to go home, and even visiting Demetrius, which might otherwise have been a fun way to burn off some energy, didn't feel right with the stain of the Atlantean artifact still upon her. So she blocked, chopped, and delivered merciless vengeance on a host of faceless and nameless opponents.

She sensed the approach easily, a sign that the other person wanted it that way. The ringing as steel cleared scabbard caused her to alter her flow, rotating toward the newcomer in time to stop her teacher's lazy diagonal chops with her swords. Ruby breathed heavily, and a note of amusement colored Keshalla's voice. "Turning to training to deal with stress. I wholeheartedly approve. Let's see how your skills are today." Her teacher delivered a front kick to Ruby's midsection, and she backpedaled to steal some of the power from the blow.

Ruby slashed her right-hand sword down in a circle block, and her opponent batted it aside with ease. Her mentor's attacks came fast, hammering at Ruby's defenses. A thread of magic coated the blades to prevent unintended cuts, but the danger of heavy impact was significant. The other woman hadn't used offensive magic yet so Ruby couldn't rely on hers for anything other than that basic protection. *Protection for her, rather than me, naturally.*

Ruby turned and dashed away on a vector that took her toward one of the boulders dotting the clearing. She leapt up, claiming the high ground, and spun to face her opponent. Keshalla gave the strategy a respectful nod, then waded in with cuts to her legs. Ruby blocked some with swords, some with boots, and whipped her sword out at her mentor's head several times.

Keshalla was almost preternatural in the way she knew when an attack was coming and could shift the targeted body part far enough out of line to avoid it. No wasted movement, complete conservation of energy. It was a technique Ruby was working on, but unless she devoted the rest of her life to daily practice, she would never reach her teacher's level. *I don't really have that kind of time. What would Demetrius say?*

She snorted internally and leapt off the boulder at the same moment the other woman jumped onto it, doubtless intending to smash her off with brute strength. Now Ruby was the one slashing and cutting at her foe's legs and failing to penetrate her seamless defense. Keshalla shifted the focus of the battle by blasting Ruby with force magic without warning, sending her stumbling backward to sprawl on the ground.

She levered herself back on her shoulders and heaved herself up to her feet, her swords interposing themselves to guide the incoming stabs out to the sides as her force shield materialized around her body. Once it was solid, she threaded a little magic into her muscles, the maximum she had so far learned how to control, to speed up her movements. Again, her teacher nodded acknowledgment of the tactic, and in an instant, had matched and exceeded her improvement.

Ruby growled under her breath, "Unfair," but kept her mind focused, defending against the incoming blows and watching for additional magical attacks. Both of her mentor's blades were like Ruby's dagger in that holding them did not preclude using magic. *I wonder if the artifact sword is like that*, she thought, followed immediately by, *and I'm a total idiot for not having asked that question already*. Her internal annoyance pushed her to fight harder, and her muscles started to protest the intensity of the workout.

The grin that tugged at the edges of her teacher's mouth

indicated that she, too, had noticed the energy drain. Naturally, she pushed faster and harder, pushing Ruby until finally, with an explosive move, Keshalla blasted both swords from her hands and delivered a jumping front kick to her chest with both feet. Ruby went flying, maintaining the presence of mind to cushion her fall with an additional buffer of force magic and lay on the ground, spent. Even the act of keeping her eyes open seemed like a herculean effort.

After several seconds, Keshalla laughed. "Are you dead, *minari?*"

"Yes. Definitely. You've finally killed me. Are you happy now? Bury me where I've fallen. Doubtless with the bodies of all your other former students."

"I believe the correct phrase for your behavior is 'drama queen.'" The other woman's smile came into view, looking down at her from above with her thumbs hooked into her weapons belt. She wore her black training armor, which Ruby now understood was far stronger than it seemed after her mentor had gifted her a set. Ruby hadn't wanted to wear hers since it reminded her of the battle after the demise of her motorcycle, and the ornate version Keshalla had provided for her *venamisha* was too pristine for practice sessions. So she was in her oldest leathers, blue and silver, and absently noted that it was time to clean them.

She forced herself into a sitting position, her stomach muscles protesting the use, and Keshalla crouched beside her. The other woman's tone held concern. "So, as much as I admire the dedication that has you here before dawn, pushing yourself to exhaustion, I have to wonder about the cause. Don't try to say diligent study because we've worked together for too long. I know that's not the reason."

Ruby couldn't hold back the snort and shook her head. "The voices in my head. From this." She tried to pull up her sleeve, but the tunic was too tight. She removed it to reveal the octopus tattoo that decorated her left forearm.

All hint of amusement left her mentor's voice. "Is that what I think it is?"

Ruby nodded. "Yes, and before you ask, accepting it wasn't voluntary. I killed its last host, and while I was down, it infected me." *Yeah, that's the right word. A virus. A parasite.*

Inside her head, the Atlantean laughed. **A partner. A master.**

Shut it. "I don't suppose you have any suggestions?"

Keshalla let out a soft growl that effectively conveyed her opinion of the artifact. "Those things are one of the reasons we chose not to engage with the wider world. They are," she paused, as if searching for the right word, then finished, "Bad."

Ruby replied with a dark laugh. "Yeah, I'm aware. He's always there, pushing against my defenses, waiting for any instant of weakness to slip his tendrils in a little deeper."

"His?"

"His. Its. Whatever. At first, the consciousness inside looked like *Mirra* Kaeni. Once I informed it that wasn't going to fly, he showed up. An Atlantean, based on everything I've seen about them. Egotistical as all hell."

Keshalla rose and extended a hand down. "Yeah, that sounds about right. I think a visit to the mystics is in order. If anyone will know more about that thing, it's them."

The head of the mystics emerged to greet them, then escorted them into the living room with its comfortable couches, tea, and trail bread. Keshalla explained the situation, and Nadar nodded. "Yes, everything we have says that was one of the arguments against interacting with the rest of Oriceran. Fear of contamination."

She rolled her eyes. "I'm right here, you know."

He gave her a small smile. "Apologies. I don't mean to be insensitive." A thoughtful look crept onto his face. "Perhaps continuing the *venamisha* will help?" The suggestion held a hopeful note.

Ruby looked at her mentor for an opinion, but Keshalla only shrugged and remained silent. "No, thanks. I have plenty of voices in my head already without offering any more of them a way in. I think we'll keep that one in reserve for now."

Nadar nodded. "Finish your tea, and I'll take you to meet the archivist. She'll have more knowledge of the artifact or know where to look for it."

The extensive library that lay below the mystics' stone home was unexpected. No rock was in evidence here, despite the area being hewn from the mountain's flesh. The walls, ceiling, and floor were all shining wood in different styles. The surface under their feet had the look of a jigsaw puzzle, with irregular pieces arranged in perfect interlock. Ornate carvings covered the ceiling, no two alike. The walls were vertical panels, a shade lighter than the floor and a touch darker than the tan surface above. All of it looked regularly polished, and the magical lights that dotted the room gave the wood an ethereal glow.

Bookshelves filled the chamber, set in perfect alignment to the walls, L-shapes to either side decreasing in size as they marched toward an empty spot in the middle. An ornate desk rested there, its wood darker than the rest. Ruby would've called it walnut but had no idea if Oriceran had walnut trees. Behind it was the oldest mystic she'd seen, a wizened Mist Elf with round glasses and grey hair, wrapped in a turtleneck sweater that seemed huge on her frail form.

The other woman dashed Ruby's initial assessment of frailty by bouncing up and walking around the desk to meet them. "Nadar, who have you brought me?" Her tone made it sound like they were a gift.

He grinned. "This is Keshalla, and this is Ruby."

The woman's eyes widened a little at the introduction of Ruby's mentor but went positively round at her name. She smiled at them both. "You are both known in these pages—Keshalla by name, Ruby by title. I was the one who found the most recent prophecy. Well, to be accurate, I was the one who made the connection. Obviously it had already been found, as it was in one of our books."

Ruby turned in a circle, admiring the space. "What are all these?" Every shelf was full although not packed. Instead, the mystics had arranged the tomes artfully, some vertically, some horizontally, some facing out so their covers were visible. Small works of art sat between them in places. She could happily spend many hours in this room, exploring its contents and uncovering its secrets.

Nadar replied dramatically, "The collected wisdom of the mystics."

The archivist snorted. "Please. They hold the history of the Mist Elves. Whenever something put into writing loses its home for one reason or another, it winds up here. We aggressively seek to preserve the remembrances of our people." Her voice turned serious. "Since you're visiting it, I can only assume it's with a purpose, as the existence of this place is one of the secrets we try not to share even with august persons such as yourselves."

Ruby nodded. "I'm seeking information about Rhazdon artifacts. Anything at all would be helpful, ideally from the perspective of one who possessed such a thing."

The archivist frowned, but it wasn't judgment. It was an effort at recall. "I have just the thing." She bustled toward the back of the room. When she returned, her hands cradled a diminutive tome, sized like a travel notebook, small enough to fit into a trouser pouch and covered with heavy leather to protect it from the rigors of the road. "This is the personal journal of the only Mist Elf I'm aware of who was host to one. The artifact was lost when he died, but the book came to us."

Ruby accepted it gratefully. "Can I repay you somehow?"

The other woman smiled. "As you continue your travels, bring back any books you think might be worth adding to our collection."

They said their goodbyes and departed, Ruby remembering the twelve-sided room and the mad Mist Elf. *Lots of books there, but I don't have any desire to get them or to let anyone else have them before thoroughly inspecting them.* Once they were outside and alone, Keshalla said, "Your face shows what you're thinking. We are *not* going back to that place, even if it's filled with books."

Ruby barked a laugh. "I thought you wanted to retire there."

Her mentor shook her head. "I've reconsidered. There's enough darkness in the surface world without voluntarily suffusing oneself in it."

She looked down at the tattoo on her arm, which seemed to shift and ripple under her inspection. "Yeah. True that."

CHAPTER FIVE

The meeting chamber was black-draped, the kemana's leader deciding that was the appropriate way to show respect for the recent events. Grentham scowled at the sight and navigated his way to an empty chair without engaging others in the room. It was both too little and too much. Too much because the magicals' loss of life during the latest incident was zero, thanks to the warning that had gone out ahead of time. Too little because it didn't acknowledge the way *everything* had changed. Gabriel Sloane had started something that wouldn't be finished quickly—revealed a dent in the armor, a vulnerability. *Now they'll be scrambling to patch it, which could be good for Aces Security or bad for the company. Either way, I need to make sure it's good for my people and me.*

The Council members were quiet as the remaining representatives assembled. Maldren gestured toward the woman beside him, and Jailynne Sunshi stood and addressed the group. "I wanted to say goodbye. I hope you understand why my family and I have to leave. Although one particular human was responsible for this, others will see it as an opportunity." Her expression was more sad than angry. "We have no desire to be caught up in it, not while our children are still young enough to be vulnerable." The people around the table offered comments of understanding and condolence, and Grentham did the same, making sure he was near the middle to be unnoticed. *Yeah, go, get whatever.* He'd never particularly liked them, and now they were irrelevant, so any need to pretend had vanished.

When she'd departed, Maldren shook his head and spoke in a grave tone. "We must always remember to balance personal needs versus community needs. On occasion, in an assembly like this, we focus too much on the group and not enough on the self. Everyone should remember that being a vibrant part of the community sometimes means leaving the community for a time, and some situations call for a permanent separation." He paused as if waiting for others to reply, but no one did. Grentham considered asking him to explain himself because he wasn't sure how leaving the community and staying in the community could coexist but chose to let it go.

Bartrak, the Kilomea, cleared his throat. "We should discuss the events in question."

Grentham immediately replied, "Agreed."

Maldren shrugged. "The purchase of the land by the trust is complete. Doubtless other interests will seek ways into it, or around it, but we are assured that no loopholes exist to allow someone from outside to interfere with our decision-making ability."

The Drow, Elnyier, asked, "Do we have any information on either of the people who were with Sloane?"

Bartrak rumbled, "Only that one was smaller than average. Maybe a gnome. Perhaps a dwarf."

Grentham snarled, "Or it could have been a short human. Given that the individual was masked, there's no way to be sure. So, let's cease casting stones. Doubtless many others were involved who weren't on the Strip that night and could be anyone. It's not impossible members of this very group might seek an advantage over the others, despite the friendly face they display in gatherings such as this." *That should diffuse the suspicion a little by increasing its scope dramatically.* It wouldn't have been his first choice of strategy, but the comment was too blatant to be ignored.

Lachsan, the Wood Elf, replied, "There is no need to search for suspicion when we have no possibility of resolving that question. What's past is past. Now, we must decide what we're going to do about it."

Rosalind Caruthers, the representative of the witches, said, "We will hire more security, for sure." Nods confirmed the others planned to do the same.

Grentham chuckled and shook his head in mild disbelief. "Have I not been suggesting that very thing for quite some time now? Perhaps *now* you'll listen, and all it required was the destruction of one of our damn casinos. My company is ready to assist. All you have to do is say the word."

Elnyier tapped the table gently to capture everyone's attention. "The Drow plan to hire additional protection as well, and I have reached out to people I know, in Kemana MountHaven and beyond. An all-magical security company from Provo has agreed to set up a satellite office here. They are shifting a significant portion of their existing workforce to Ely and will hire replacements to work for their existing clients. That way, we can be assured that if we contract their personnel, those individuals have a history that demonstrates loyalty and reliability."

Grentham snorted. "I'm sure that means they're *completely* trustworthy and could *never* be bought off by anyone with deep pockets." He shook his head again. "As always, I believe you should trust one of your own, namely me and my company. But you'll make whatever choices you'll make, as you have in the past. If you choose poorly, let's hope no one else pays for your foolishness. Speaking of which, maybe a bigger priority at the moment is to determine how to keep more of our casinos from falling."

The chide earned him scowls from the others in the room, although their host's expression remained neutral as he spoke. "The Paranormal Defense Agency has deployed in greater force as a result of the event. I have been in contact with them, and they are taking it upon themselves to increase surveillance to identify potential trouble."

Challen, the Gnome healer, replied, "I've seen many more drones buzzing around on the streets above. Is that what you mean?"

Maldren nodded. "That's part of it. They tell me they're also bringing in more operatives, planning to do what they call a 'serious sweep' of magical crime in the city."

Grentham replied, "Correct me if I'm wrong here, but Gabriel Sloane was human, wasn't he? A bit outside the PDA's normal mandate."

Their host shrugged. "Apparently, that mandate has

expanded, in their estimation." Worried looks greeted that statement, and he acknowledged them with a frown. "I agree this is a matter of concern. We must be vigilant, keep our eyes open, and watch both those in need of protection and those who are allegedly acting as our protectors."

Grentham grumbled, "Like those three who could've prevented all this mess simply by giving themselves up." He shook his head again and raised a hand before anyone could argue. "I know. It was an insane request in the first place, and no one should've given in to it. But, if we are watching the protectors, we must consider that trio as well. Who knows what's really going on with them? Hell, for all we know, the whole thing was an elaborate ruse of some kind, for purposes we can't yet identify."

The Atlantean representative to the Council, Andrielle, scowled. "Are you truly suggesting Gabriel Sloane sacrificed himself for a fiction? That may be the dumbest thing ever said at this table."

Grentham fired back, "Of course not. Obviously, things didn't go as Sloane had planned. But who knows? Could've been a double-cross. My point is, we *don't* have a clear understanding of it, and thus we have to be careful trusting anyone who's not us."

Rayar Achera changed the subject. "At Spirits, we've installed new technologies to assist in protecting the casino. Our entry scanners now detect metal, explosives, illicit drugs, and the presence of magic. They were expensive and only exist because we as a group agreed some time ago to help fund the research and development of the technology, which seems downright prescient given the current circumstance. The company assures me they can provide them at cost to our casinos. The price of that assistance is renegotiation of the contract to allow them to open up to other markets faster than we'd originally planned. I see no problem with this arrangement and hope you'll support it."

Maldren asked for objections, but none came. He said, "This is a prime example of what we can accomplish when we work together, both toward the success of the Kemana and the success of the city above us. We will have several weighty issues on the agenda for the next meeting, including initial plans for the space once filled by the Mist. I ask you all to remember that you are collaborators more than you are competitors. At its heart, Magic City is a community, and it's up to us to remember to act like neighbors rather than opponents."

The rest of the meeting passed in a haze of mundane issues Grentham participated in with only a minimal allocation of his brainpower. The rest sorted through strategies and tactics, ultimately coming up with nothing certain. When they had been working directly for Sloane, certainty was present. It was wrapped in danger and carried the man's constant condescension, but the path forward was clearly visible. *For a few steps, anyway. Now, we're walking sightlessly in the dark, and monsters abound. Time to do another review of my people to make sure there's no enemy hidden among the loyal ones.*

CHAPTER SIX

Morrigan Achera crouched on the edge of a three-story rooftop and gazed down at the street below. She and Idryll had made a habit of nighttime patrols since the incident on the Strip. The ambient sense of danger in Ely had ratcheted up considerably, and she saw it expressed in the actions of the people on the streets. They stayed in groups and moved more quickly from place to place. Someone who hadn't spent as much time as she had watching and characterizing people's behavior might not have noticed it, but the evidence was undeniable. Magic City had changed, and not for the better. She muttered, "Well, we'll have to figure out how to change it back."

From her right, where the tiger-woman crouched, Idryll asked, "Change what back?"

"Nothing. I mean, everything. Never mind."

Her companion laughed. "Every time I think you might have avoided whatever damaged your sister's brain, you say something like that. I'm filled with concern."

Morrigan grinned. Making fun of Ruby was one of the

games they both deeply enjoyed, whether she was physically present or not, and the insults occupied a decent portion of their time on patrol. "Yeah, yeah. Trust me. Unless I start sniffing glue, I shouldn't have any issues similar to hers." She nodded at a pair of people below. Human males, wearing leather jackets, thick boots, and chains dangling from their belts. "Looks like we have some street gang wannabes down there."

Idryll's nostrils flared as if she smelled them as well as saw them. "Or real ones, maybe. The way they move isn't all false confidence."

"Think we should follow?"

"Definitely."

As they traveled along the rooftops, hidden under veils and keeping a close eye on their quarry, Morrigan asked, "Do you think we need to worry about the thing in Ruby's arm?" She'd done some research on artifacts but hadn't come up with much useful information about coping with having one.

Idryll's tone was an answer in itself. "Absolutely. Everything I've ever heard about those things says they're trouble."

Morrigan's thoughts shifted back into the moment as the duo below met up with another pair, their numbers redoubling shortly thereafter. "Okay, this is starting to look like an actual gang. What do you think those chuckleheads are up to?" The men continued to move with seeming purpose, headed away from the Strip and into the lower rent businesses at the edge of town.

Idryll replied, "Predators."

Morrigan nodded. "Yeah, my thought too. What are they hunting?"

"Anything that comes across their path, probably."

She moved faster, hoping to spot any potential victims before the gang could take action. Morrigan tensed as the group passed a small gaggle of tourists who were making their way from club to club, brave ones who had ventured off the Strip. *Although, I guess being on the Strip these days is itself kind of an act of bravery. We definitely* do *need to change things back.*

Idryll hissed. "Trouble."

The gang members had turned into an alley, and a single individual occupied that narrow lane. From the perspective of her lofty perch, Morrigan saw white hair and dark skin, the frequent telltales of a Drow elf. She'd extended her bow when the gang's numbers grew and now pulled an arrow from her quiver and set it loosely to the string. "That doesn't look promising. I'll hit the ones in the back. Then we'll go after the ones in the front.

The tiger-woman sounded eager to mix it up. "Got it."

The gang neared the figure, which slowed to a stop. The human in the lead called, "Hey, pointy. Kind of late for you to be out all by yourself, isn't it?"

His tone didn't quite promise violence other than the verbal kind. Morrigan drew and aimed at the wall opposite, in the space between the last two ranks of two. The Dark Elf's answer filtered up, soft but calm. "There's no need for trouble. You can step aside and let me continue on my way."

The group laughed and stopped moving. Their mouthpiece said, "You want us to press up against the sides, and you'll walk through the middle? Is that it?"

"That would be acceptable."

"I have a better idea. How about you turn around and go back the way you came." Murmurs of support rose from behind him.

An inappropriate level of confusion entered the Drow male's voice, suggesting he played with the humans in the alley. "Then how would I get where I'm going?"

The human gave an expansive shrug. "Not my concern. Now move, or we're coming through you."

The gang didn't wait for him to comply. The front rank surged forward, and Morrigan released her arrow an instant later. In her peripheral vision, Idryll leapt from the building, headed for the space between the first and second ranks. Below, the supposed victim moved quickly, and the glint of moonlight on metal shone in his hands. Morrigan cursed and reached back for another arrow, realizing the situation was about to spiral out of control.

Three stories was an easy drop for Idryll, not even requiring a roll to dissipate her momentum. She landed in a crouch and immediately whipped her foot around in a sweep kick, aiming for the gang members nearest the Drow. Her foot connected with the heel of one, sending him stumbling against the wall to his left but missed the other. The Drow taking responsibility for his defense informed her next move, which was to turn toward the second rank with a mocking grin.

The one nearest, on her right, threw himself forward with his arms stretched wide to tackle her, trying to use his greater bulk to his advantage in the narrow space. She could've stabbed him with her claws easily, raking his flesh from throat to stomach in the time it would take him to close, but leaving bodies on the streets was not a good plan. *Or so Ruby keeps saying.* She met him with a kick instead, her knee coming up to her chest and her foot pistoning out. The blow caught him in the sternum, and he coughed and sagged against the wall to her right, unable to breathe.

The other one used her focus on the first to whip a chain at her head, and Idryll crouched to avoid it. That enemy had stepped back into an acceptable fighting stance, and she grinned. "Oh, you fancy yourself a fighter, then? Let's see what you've got."

The initial arrow she'd sent was the sonic one she'd last used on the Strip. It dropped the two rearmost immediately. The other two staggered forward, outside the range of the assault on their inner ears. *Dammit, I need to talk to Kayleigh about making that more powerful.* Her fingers found the explosive arrow, then she reconsidered and selected the knockout gas. She hadn't chosen that at the start out of concern for the Drow, but given the escalation, figured that if everyone in the alley succumbed, she could still clean them up and help the victim later. Idryll's mask would protect her for long enough to finish things. She loosed the arrow, and it sped toward the middle of the group.

When it struck, the clouds billowed out, and another gang member fell. The gas flowed suddenly away as if someone had cast a spell to dissipate it. *What the hell?* She selected a lightning arrow and fired at the chest of the next rearmost. The magic exploded on impact and dropped him to the ground, jerking and writhing. Then things were too close so she hit the button to retract her bow and leapt for the alley floor.

Idryll leaned aside to dodge the slash of the chain, which was far heavier than it had first appeared, and stepped back to avoid the backhand follow-up. She darted in and punched, but the man brought his left arm across in a quick block. His left foot licked out, and she twisted so it caught her on the thigh rather than the knee, staying close to nullify the chain. He hammered his right hand at her head, and she blocked the strike easily. The chain whipped around to smack her in the back but lacked force due to her proximity, rendering it nothing more than a nuisance.

His face twisted in anger, and he snapped his head forward, going for a headbutt. She had no way to avoid it completely, so she lowered her chin, taking the blow above her forehead. The impact momentarily dazed them both, but she was quicker to recover. A punch with her left, another with her right, and a kick through the space that the strikes opened sent the man flying backward into another near him. At the sound of choking and gurgling behind her, she turned to discover the Drow had stabbed the one she'd tripped in the neck, and the wounded man was slumped on the ground, his hands clasped over the bleeding hole. An equally fatal strike took out the other one in the front rank, a wicked spin kick snapping his neck with a loud *crack*. She shouted, "Stop, it's under control."

———

Morrigan landed and was momentarily distracted by Idryll's exclamation. She laid about with fists and elbows, taking down the remaining humans in a rush from behind. When they were all down, dazed or unconscious, she stepped beside her partner to face the Drow. "Why did you kill them?"

The Dark Elf's face was sharp-boned and handsome, a little longer than average. She couldn't help but think his lips were pretty, but the words that came out of them were definitely not. "They earned their fate. This is *our* city, and humans have no right to attempt to exert their will upon us here."

Idryll shook her head. "And yet, simply injuring them would have sufficed." She gestured at the surviving gang members.

The elf flicked the black metal blades to clear the blood from them and slid them into sheaths on either hip. "That sort of thinking solves nothing. It only perpetuates the problem. My way, you see, eliminates the problem."

Morrigan rested her hands on her dagger hilts. "Until their friends come along to take revenge."

He shrugged. "Then I will kill their friends."

She sighed and shook her head. "And when *their* friends arrive?"

"They, too, shall die."

Morrigan answered, "We can't allow that."

Idryll confirmed, "We cannot."

He gave them a lazy smile. "Pick a side, strangers. If you choose the one opposite me, know that you will receive the same treatment as the humans." The thought of trying to capture the Drow had barely entered her mind when the man waved, and a wall of smoke appeared between them. She charged through, but when she got to the other side, he was gone. "Damn. That's not good."

Idryll stepped beside her. "You did say you wanted change."

"Yeah, but not to make it worse." She shook her head. "Ruby's going to blame this on me. I know it."

CHAPTER SEVEN

Jared Trenton scowled as the coffee overflowed the side of the cup and scalded his hand. "Ow, damn." He laughed. "If that isn't a metaphor for the current situation, being in hot water and getting burned, I don't know what is." He finished extending the drink to his partner without spilling it further.

Grentham, dressed as always in all-black and wearing an expression to match, nodded and took it carefully from him. "Right? Things are definitely topsy-turvy nowadays."

The quiet room at Aces Security was state-of-the-art but decidedly light on creature comforts. Two plastic chairs, a metal table, and white surfaces all around. They'd built it as a floating chamber, with none of the internal structure directly touching the outer except through a layer of signal- and sound-absorbing panels. They'd tested it extensively, and no microphone they had access to could pick anything up from beyond its walls. It was okay to bring their phones inside since the room eliminated those signals as well. They'd also warded it against magical detection. Jared fell into the chair with a sigh. "How about the new one?"

His partner nodded. "Yeah, that Thompson is tough. She's more than a match for Smith, I'd say."

The additional representative from their boss's wife— *now the new boss, I guess*—had shown up with the more familiar one to lay down the law. Jared asked, "So if our goal is now to 'move aggressively to acquire or take out the other companies,' where should we start?" He emphasized the word aggressive, just like Thompson had during their interview.

Grentham snorted. "Well, some news from the Council meeting last night might influence that decision a bit. Apparently, Worldspan Security is setting up shop in town. All magicals, so they already have an inside track. Bloody Elnyier and her Drow contacts."

"You have a thing against the Drow, don't you?"

His partner shrugged. "On a personal level, they're generally no better or worse than anyone else. They seem to utilize their network a lot more effectively than any of the other immigrants from Oriceran. Most have their hands in trade of one kind or another, and they've spread out to pretty much everywhere. Smart move, really. I wish my people had been that clever."

"I know this is only a human's opinion, but it seems like the Drow tend to be more loners than other magicals."

"That's my perception as well. However, since I'm not a Drow, who the hell knows? Anyway, their entry onto the playing field has to be our first concern, and maybe our second and third, too."

Jared sipped his coffee for several moments, thinking

through the potential plays. "It'll be difficult to take them out with the people we have at hand."

"I agree. We should make a peaceful overture. A partnership or a buyout would be the best options. We still have the gems we didn't commit to the trap to sell if we need quick cash." He gestured toward the small container in the corner. The diamonds lived in the secure room, as they both thought that the magicals might have some way to track them. "If we have to go with a less peace-loving option, I can get some people together."

Jared decided it was time to bring everything out into the light. "From your side gig, you mean."

Grentham nodded. "Yeah. They're trustworthy, which is the most important thing. Not the sharpest tools in the kit, but that's okay. With the right leadership from our regulars, they'll be able to get the job done, or at least harry the defense enough that our people can make it happen. We should probably lay in a bunch of anti-magic bullets."

Jared winced but nodded. "Yeah, you're right. I'll see what the black market in Vegas has to offer." Their official supply would have had no recent reason to be diminished, so they couldn't visibly add to it. Jared wasn't positive the government kept an eye on such things, but he also wasn't convinced they didn't, and it was better to maintain a low profile wherever possible. He chuckled. "Think the Drow network could hook me up with that?"

Grentham scowled. "I doubt it. They're too busy collecting the best artifacts and magical items."

"Still raw about the thing with Goryo?"

His partner gave a single sharp nod. "That bastard

Sloane had to go and die before he could even pay me for the artifact, which is now lost forever."

"Or at least until we kill the person it's bonded to."

"Since we don't know who they are, that doesn't seem particularly likely right at the moment. Still, I'm always open to opportunities as they come up."

He laughed. "Okay, then. Any reason to wait, or should we go have a visit with the new team in town?"

Grentham grinned. "Let me grab some supplies from the equipment room, then yeah, I think we should give them an appropriate welcome to Magic City."

Worldspan had rented out an overly large office building in a complex nearby. It was a guarded community, unlike their own, with a single entrance and exit commanded by a guard post. As he piloted the SUV up to the shack and rolled down the window, Jared muttered, "Rent-a-cop is human." He raised his voice and said, "Hi, Jared Trenton, Aces Security. Here to see Angelina Prash."

The guard nodded. "You're on the list. Go on through. First building on your right."

As if I didn't already know that. He plastered a fake smile on his face. "Thanks, buddy." When the window closed, he observed, "Pistol and taser. Assault rifle on the wall. Computer terminal."

Grentham peered down at his phone, entering information. "Got all that except for the rifle. I'll need to reach out and get someone to check the cybersecurity. I know we have people, but the infomancer Goryo used seemed really sharp."

"Agreed. Time to outsource."

His partner snapped pictures with his phone as they drove toward the site, reconnaissance in case they had to go with the harder option. When they arrived, both men dropped their phones into the secure signal-blocking compartment in the armrest, and Jared activated the vehicle's security when they stepped out. The protection it gave the stuff inside the car was impressive, but even better was the 360-degree surveillance from tiny cameras mounted around the car. The feed was immediately linked back to their base, so if anyone did mess with the vehicle, they'd know about it.

A short sidewalk led to the lobby, which was impersonal and industrial. A semicircular desk enclosed two guards, both standing with hands out of sight but arms bent in such a way that they were probably near weapons. The pair of elves nodded at their entrance after buzzing them in. The dark-haired one on the left said, "Mr. Trenton, Mr. Grentham, welcome. An escort will be with you shortly." He inclined his head toward a set of couches set at right angles around a coffee table in the corner.

Jared nodded and sauntered in the indicated direction. He kept his eyes forward, but his expansive gaze took in the obvious defenses. Security cameras, a metal detector at least, set into the doorway that led from the lobby. Only one entry into the room from the outside, and only the one visible exit leading farther into the building. They didn't have time to sit before a Kilomea, muscular even for its kind, came through the door from the interior. He was tall enough that his hair brushed against the doorframe top. "Gentlemen," he rumbled, "come this way."

They followed him obediently into the building's interior but only had a short walk to a conference room. *Smart, not letting anyone too far inside.* The place smelled new, looked mostly unused, and additional signs of recent occupation were apparent in the crates stacked in offices visible through corporate glass walls. The conference room was also surrounded by a transparent border, revealing an oval table big enough to seat ten or twelve. Only one person was present, a Wood Elf female, reclining in an expensive-looking chair with her feet up on the table. Thin blonde-brown braids reached toward the floor from her reclined position. Her clothes weren't in the least formal: all leather, black pants, and a red tank top-like thing that left her muscular arms bare.

As they stepped into the room, she swept her calf-high boots down and rose to greet them, extending a hand. "Hello, gentlemen. I wondered which of the local companies would be the first to grace our halls. I'm Angelina, principal of this office of Worldspan Security."

They shook hands in turn, introducing themselves, and moved toward the nearest seats when she gestured for them to do so. Hilts of knives were in easy reach on each of her hips, and a pistol rode in a drop holster on her right leg, the tie-down strap reassuringly in place. *Even so, if she's anywhere near as competent as she looks, she could shoot us as fast as breathing.* The woman's face was beautiful in the ethereal way that many elves' were, but the perfection was interrupted by a thin scar that ran along a cheekbone. He found it increased her attractiveness rather than the opposite. She said, "Let's not waste one another's time. What is it you want?"

Jared shrugged. "As you wish. We're open to creating a partnership with you here in Ely."

A thin smile appeared. "We're always willing to consider subcontractors if they meet our highly exacting standards."

Grentham laughed, and it sounded genuine. "Not quite the arrangement we had in mind. More the other way around. You're new here, so you probably don't understand how things work."

She echoed him, and it, too, sounded unfeigned. "We've done our research, gentlemen. We're aware of your position and equally aware of the existing firms' collective inability to protect the casinos and their owners. That's why we were asked to come here, to supply what you so clearly lack. I'm afraid you've made the trip for nothing. We're not interested in alliance or partnership. Let's consider ourselves professional colleagues who stay out of each other's way, and all will be well."

The dwarf bristled. "And if that's not adequate to our needs?"

She shrugged. "Let the competition begin. We've outlasted any number of other companies during our rise, and yours would be barely a footnote on that list. By all means, do your best to steal our clients, and we'll do our best to steal yours. At the end of the day, I'm completely confident in the outcome of that game. Can you say the same?"

Jared shook his head and rose. "Well, enough said, I guess. Thanks for your time. It's good to put a face to a name, at least. Your reputation precedes you." They had done their research, and the woman across from them was one of the company's founding members. For her to take over the Ely operation in person showed how serious Worldspan was about their expansion.

Prash leaned back, returned her feet to the table, and nodded. "Same in reverse. I wish you luck, gentlemen. The more you get in our way, the more you're going to need it."

The Kilomea arrived to escort them out. When they had left the office complex in the rearview, Jared asked, "Did you leave the bugs behind?"

Grentham laughed. "Everywhere we visited. When we activate them tonight, we should get some useful intel." The devices were crawlers, super small and capable of only three things: concealment, locomotion, and sending audio and video signals. Quality was an issue, but they had been meticulously engineered to encode in a way that reduced transmission bandwidth as long as one had the proper decoder on the far end. "When the time comes, we'll be ready. Then we'll see who needs luck and who doesn't."

CHAPTER EIGHT

Ruby and Demetrius stepped through the portal Daphne created to take them to Vegas. The witch madly grinned as Ruby turned to thank her, and she rolled her eyes. "Thanks, appreciate the help."

"You kids have fun." The other woman's voice was full of amusement. In truth, Ruby had possessed no idea how bubbly and happy her lab partner could get before setting her up with the gig at Spirits. She found the freedom to research deeply enjoyable, and happiness oozed from her.

Ruby turned to Demetrius with a sigh as the rift closed. "Well, at least she's happy, right?"

He laughed. "Absolutely." Her boyfriend looked downright delicious in a dark suit and open-collared button-down shirt, and while she always found him attractive, she had been more than impressed to see how well he cleaned up.

She was in a sapphire and silver dress with actual heels. Low heels, since they were more practical and she wasn't as agile on any over three inches high, but heels nonetheless. Their magical transport had deposited them a couple of blocks away from their destination, and they strolled toward it, small talk filling the time comfortably. It was their first real date, and Ruby had called in every favor she was owed to make it special and promised a few more. *Maybe I can overwhelm him with so much impressive stuff he won't notice my broken brain.* Even the voices in her head were quiet at the moment though, something for which she was deeply grateful.

They stepped onto the Strip and headed for the nearest casino. It was home to the hottest new restaurant in town —a Drow-owned establishment called Midnight. It was impossible to get a reservation, and the line of hopefuls praying for a cancellation was twenty deep outside the place. She walked up to the black-robed, white-haired Dark Elf at the entrance and said, "Achera, for two."

The hostess nodded and gave her a bright smile. "Right this way." The restaurant's interior was done up like a night sky, with only enough illumination to avoid tripping over things. Each table was a star, courtesy of a small glowing prism set as a centerpiece. Their arrangement had no apparent logic unless you understood the magic incorporated in the design. She sensed the spells at work and didn't doubt that even mundane humans would notice something.

The result was an atmosphere of anticipation, with a hint of potential danger in the darkness. *Only enough to make it a unique experience*, she figured. They entered the kitchen, which was as bright as the outer area had been dark. The chef's table was in a corner, behind a transparent panel that allowed its occupants to watch everything while providing sufficient quiet that they would feel more or less alone. As they sat, glasses of champagne appeared at the table in the hands of the head chef. He smiled. "Ruby, so wonderful to see you."

She stood, took the drinks, and wrapped him in a hug. "Same to you, Merten." Demetrius had also risen, and she introduced him. "Demetrius is my boyfriend. Merten is an old friend of Margrave's."

The Dark Elf nodded. "Phineas helped with the prisms outside. When he asked if we could find an opening for you, it was of course my pleasure to do so. Now, relax, and you'll get to try a little of almost everything on the menu."

They sat, and Ruby explained, "The chef's table here basically involves getting a bit of whatever is cooked tonight in the restaurant. So, it's a completely different experience every time you come, or so I've heard. I've never been here." She was excited about the meal and more excited to be sharing it with her boyfriend. "A few things are guaranteed, even if they don't get ordered. Including the whole dessert menu, if we so desire."

Demetrius laughed. "I always wanted to marry rich. I could get used to this."

She shook her head. "First, *I'm* not used to this kind of living, so maybe don't count your chickens on that one. Also, it's a little early to be talking about marriage, don't you think?"

He sipped his champagne and shrugged. "If the food is as good as this drink, no, it's really not." They laughed together. *Totally not ready to tie the knot, but I like that you're considering it, even jokingly.*

The first course arrived, a scallop for each of them

presented with a delicious sauce on a teardrop-shaped plate. They sampled it, and her eyes rolled from pleasure. "Okay, maybe I could get used to this."

They tried several more dishes, then Demetrius said, "You know, I was wondering. Is it hard for you to keep up the disguise?"

She patted her lips with a napkin and took a sip of the red wine that had appeared with the third appetizer. "Honestly, no. I've been doing it for so long that it's automatic. I rarely think about it unless there's something nearby that might cause it to fail."

He nodded. "I've noticed you don't even let it go when you're, uh, distracted." A little thrill shot through her belly at the thought of his distractions. He was *very* good at them. "But, you know, I'd like to see you for real."

She lifted an eyebrow, and half-teasing, countered, "This *is* real."

He chuckled. "Okay, for fake then. Whatever. Your other form."

"Not here, but sure, sometime soon we can do that."

He replied, "Speaking of the future, what do you think will happen to Magic City after all the recent unpleasantness?"

She shrugged. "The town's faced challenges before, and doubtless we'll face them again. Overall, it's a few bumps in the road, I imagine."

"Pretty big bumps."

She laughed. "Yeah, that's fair to say. I mean, the Council has plans, and they're more or less united, so I don't think there's a huge risk of the place falling apart. Obviously, security everywhere will have to be tighter."

He scowled. "I saw all the drones flying around last time I was on the Strip. Kind of breaks the mood a little."

"I'm working on a version of my drone with improved camouflage. Maybe I can sell them to Magic City."

"Sounds right." Their conversation paused for the delivery of a small salad for them to share featuring greens, cheese, fruit, and nuts. "So, do you think you'll stay?"

Ruby nodded. "I do. At first, I thought I'd only be home for a while. Still, I like it, and I feel as if I belong here. Well, there."

He lowered his voice and put his hand up to his mouth nonchalantly so that no one in the kitchen could read his lips. "Are you being careful enough to make that a long-term thing?"

The subject of her actions as Magic City's defender didn't come up that often, by some unspoken agreement, and it felt weird to hear the question. "I hope so. After all, knowing that you clean up this well, I need to stick around for more dates. Not to mention that now *you* owe *me* one."

The rest of the meal passed in a blur of gastronomic delight. The main courses started with lobster in a sweet sauce that seemed like it shouldn't work but did. After that, a cut of beef from Japan was literally melt-in-the-mouth tender. More, each item was unique and deeply enjoyable. The culinary barrage finished with six different kinds of cakes, three for each of them, and coffees flavored with a syrup from Oriceran, a taste that hadn't yet come to Earth in any other way.

When they were well and truly stuffed, Merten gave them a kitchen tour and instruction on what all the stations did. Afterward, they headed for the exit. Halfway there, she turned him toward the casino elevators. He laughed. "I must *really* look good. I didn't realize how attractive I can be."

Ruby slapped him on the arm. "We're not going to a room, fool." Instead, their destination was the club on the top of the hotel tower. It was an outdoor venue, full of music, bright lights that threw colors into the darkness, and a huge pool filled with scantily clad men and women from both planets. They danced for a while, and when she was ready for a rest, she dragged him over to a corner table. She ordered the club's signature drink called Night's Fire, a mixture of caffeine and liquor that tasted like perfection.

He gestured at the surrounding people. "Why don't we have this sort of thing in Magic City?"

She shrugged. "Lots of reasons, I guess. This town is a lot older than ours, so we're pretty much at the starting gate in comparison. It requires a certain level of tourists to make a place like this work." She leaned forward, and he brought his head down near hers. "Think about it, probably at least a dozen of these parties are going on right now, all filled to the brim because they have to be for the profit margin to work out. That's a ton of revelers." He nodded. "Plus, we can't compete with Sin City on its terms. Replicating what they do well isn't a good competitive position. We have to change the game."

"So that's why the idea of putting a Fremont Street-like canopy over the Strip was a nonstarter?"

Her father had told her about the discussion, and she had shared it with her boyfriend. "Exactly. We're better off doubling down on what we do differently instead of trying to copy what works here. Although, I think this drink might have to come back with us." She kissed him on the nose and emptied her glass. He laughed and pulled her onto the dance floor again.

An hour later, hot, sweaty, and entranced by the night, she dragged him back to the elevator. "Now we go to the hotel room." His mouth fell open in surprise, and she laughed. "What? You can't look like that and *not* expect me to jump on you."

They made it through the bedroom door before falling on one another, hot and heavy kisses and groping hands only broken when she pushed him away. "Okay, you asked for it." She let the illusion fade, showing him her slightly altered features, the pointed ears the most telling difference. To judge by his reaction and what followed, he didn't find them problematic in the least.

A few hours later, she was awake in bed, staring at the ceiling as wild thoughts tumbled through her brain. His voice was a surprise as he quietly asked, "Do you realize you're rubbing your arm?"

She looked down to see he was correct, that her fingers were compulsively working over the tattoo. She shook her head. "Sorry to wake you."

"That's not the problem. The problem is you don't seem to have come to terms with that, or with how you got it, or whatever."

She sighed. "It's hard. The thing is a constant presence in the back of my mind unless I'm guarding carefully against it or well-distracted."

He laughed. "I'm happy to help with the second part

whenever I can, but I don't think that's a viable solution overall. I'm willing to try it if you are."

She smacked him gently. "I'm planning to talk to some people about dealing with it when my schedule allows it."

He replied, "Make time. Seriously."

She grinned and twisted fully toward him. "Promise. I'll do it as soon as I reasonably can. For tonight, I'm afraid I'm going to need almost constant distraction. Got any ideas?" His answer was a kiss that turned into much, much more.

CHAPTER NINE

The opportunity to train with Sheen and her agents had been so hard to schedule that Ruby wasn't willing to delay it, not even to spend another day in a hotel room with Demetrius. They portaled home, she showered and dressed, and it was off to meet Cara in the kemana to portal to their base.

Diana and Rath greeted them as they arrived, the troll and Idryll engaging in a complicated set of fist bumps and hand slaps. Morrigan shook her head. She whispered, "Your tiger partner is crazy."

Ruby laughed and also shook her head. Diana said, "Let's get to the fun stuff." The agent escorted them to a large room filled with a bunch of white cubes stacked several stories high. She explained, "This is our training chamber. Basically, the computer can generate random or specific tactical situations, and the blocks move around to create them for us. I've chosen a random one today."

Two people Ruby hadn't met before were in the locker area at the front of the room, donning some sort of science-fiction-looking armor. Diana introduced them. "This is Anik, and this is Tony. Along with Cara and Rath, they're going to be the opposition. I'll work with you three. If we have time left over after the first run, and we're all up for it, the teams will switch up for the second one. You can take lockers six, seven, and eight."

Ruby opened hers and found boots, pants, tunic, and a helmet that covered her whole face. Putting them on was like slipping into a tight pair of jeans, but with a strange metallic chiming as the individual scales flexed and shifted. It was easy to move in, far more than one would expect. She said, "Okay, I'll bite. What the hell is this stuff? More importantly, did you get it from Tony Stark? Even more importantly, if so, can I meet him?"

Morrigan shook her head. "Try not to make us look stupid in front of the agents for once, Ruby."

Idryll added, "I don't think she's intellectually capable of that."

Ruby stuck out her tongue at her partners as Diana replied, "This is training armor. It registers hits and incapacitates the affected areas by freezing the scales in that location. It doesn't give you the pain of the wound, but it does a pretty good job of simulating the immobility the damage would cause. It's not *Avengers* gear, unfortunately. I've always wanted to meet Scarlett Johansson. Instead, it came from a defense contractor. They're working on it for the Army, but it's still too expensive to roll out. They were amenable to supplying some prototypes after the right level of begging. Of course, they get free research in return."

Idryll complained, "I'm not a fan. This is very tight."

Ruby replied, "Well, I guess anything would be when you spend most of your time walking around naked."

"Fur is not naked."

Morrigan added, "I'm afraid I have to go with Ruby on this one, Idryll."

The shapeshifter scowled, baring her teeth. "Idiots. You're jealous, as always."

Diana laughed. "Okay, so weapons. I'll be taking my usual rifle and pistol. Do y'all want to give rifles a try?" All three of them shook their heads simultaneously, and the agent smiled at them. "Pistols for you too, then. How about shock gloves for you, Idryll?"

"No claws allowed?"

"Definitely not. The goal here is training, not wounding or killing. Oh, and no magic."

Ruby groaned. "I think the opposing force has a definite advantage, then."

Rath, who had donned his suit with impressive speed, jumped up onto the bench and struck a pose. "We shall fight on the beaches. We shall fight on the landing grounds. We shall never surrender."

Diana shook her head. "Where did you see that?"

"*Darkest Hour*. Gary Oldman."

"You know, not every real-life movie truly shows real life accurately."

"I disbelieve."

Cara closed her locker with a *clang* and laughed. "Ever since we got him playing *Dungeons & Dragons* with us, his first response to everything is to disbelieve. To be fair, he's figured out a couple of traps that way. It doesn't work quite as well outside the game."

The troll's grin widened. "It will. Just you wait and see."

Diana handed over their choices and gave Idryll a thin belt that held the battery for her gloves. "Okay, secondary weapons. I'll have my sword. What do you want?"

Ruby replied, "Sword." Morrigan opted for daggers, Idryll chose nothing, and moments later they were fully geared up. Their opponents waved goodbye and headed into the interior of the modular structure. Only one opening led inside, but Diana assured them it would be far more complex inside than they probably expected. "Whoever programmed the thing did a fantastic job with it. I think this will eventually wind up being the best and only unit for training Special Forces operatives. Fortunately, we're lucky enough to have it first."

Ruby asked, "Benefits of a good relationship with the government?"

Diana snorted. "Good might be a strong word. Let's just say my boss, Bryant, is really effective at convincing people to let us try things out for them. He's a hell of a politician. For a former field agent, anyway."

After the appropriate amount of time, they slipped on their helmets and headed in. Diana led their single-file line as the head of the team, followed by Idryll, Ruby, and Morrigan. Her sister complained, "Feels weird to be without my bow."

The agent replied, "We tried to brainstorm a way this training session would work with the bow, but it's too close quarters. For that one, eventually, we'll likely have to do something outdoors. However, you've given Kayleigh a project to think about, which keeps her out of trouble, mostly. Enduring a bored tech is not a thing you want to do often."

When they turned a corner to discover an opening ahead, Diana stopped them with a raised fist. "Okay, here's how this will work. I'll go in fast and hard. Idryll, since you'll need to be up close to fight, you'll charge any opposition. If you find multiples and have to choose, head for the one with the heaviest weapon. As far as positioning, I'll go straight and veer left or right as the situation dictates. Morrigan, you go left as soon as you clear the entry. Ruby, you go right. This will be our standard deployment unless I say different."

Morrigan said, "Why, if it's okay to ask?"

Diana's smile was audible. "It wouldn't be on an op, but learning is what training is all about. This positioning ensures we'll have separate lines of fire as long as we don't do anything stupid. Idryll needing to be hand-to-hand adds an unpredictable factor, so she'll need to be ready to drop to the ground if anyone yells 'down.'"

The shapeshifter, uncommonly serious, replied, "Got it."

Their suits had external pickups and excellent optics and acoustics, so even while entombed inside, everything sounded more or less like it would normally have. The only difference was that Ruby couldn't feel the atmosphere on her face and could only smell the metal and plastic of the helmet. Diana said, "Okay. Here we go," and surged into the room.

Ruby followed the others through into the chamber beyond, which was two stories high, as opposed to the claustrophobic nature of the corridor they'd been in. One opponent was visible, their rifle already aimed at Idryll, who was running straight for them. Diana had moved off to the left, and Ruby took a step to her right as instructed and brought up her pistol. Their enemy shot first, and Idryll dodged to the side and rolled, a yelp of surprise heralding a likely hit from their foe. Ruby, Morrigan, and Diana all opened up simultaneously, and the attacker staggered and fell under the barrage.

Diana ordered, "Morrigan, guard the exit. Ruby, help Idryll." Then their leader walked over and shook her head at the figure on the floor. "So, they decided to sacrifice you, Tony?"

Whoever controlled their comms must've been watching because his voice came over the same earpiece that had formerly been her team only. "I lost rock paper scissors. Pretty sure I took out your tiger, though, which would be a more than fair trade."

Idryll, who Ruby had helped to a sitting position, replied, "My leg is locked up. I think he must've hit me in the knee."

Tony groaned. "I was aiming for your chest. That was a great dodge. You should really carry a weapon, though."

"Or maybe I should stay in the back, then attack by surprise once things get started. Ruby can be the one who runs in as a distraction. That's her best role. Bait."

Diana's helmet bobbed. "Yep, I agree on the surprise attack. We'll try that on the next go-round whenever we do one. Figuring stuff out is the whole purpose of this exercise. For the moment, though, you'll be in spectator mode so you can watch."

Idryll replied, "I'm able to limp along."

"No, you're a liability if you do. In a real operation, we'd probably have to give you medical attention right now and definitely couldn't detail someone to help you continue forward. So, you're out."

"Well, damn."

Ruby laughed and patted the shapeshifter on the shoulder as she rose to her feet. "That's okay. We'll give them hell in round two."

They advanced down the only available hallway with Diana's rifle leading the way. She stopped again before stepping through the next opening. "Okay, we'll do the same thing, only I'll go up the middle and stay there. Morrigan has the left. Ruby, you're on the right." They rushed in and found nothing in front of them. Diana spun and brought her rifle up, pointing it toward the ceiling, and at the same moment, Morrigan went down, crying out in surprise. Ruby turned in time to see a blur go past as Rath, who had apparently hidden up high, raced by, headed for the exit.

Diana said, "Oh no, you don't," and shifted to block him. He flipped a throwing knife that required her to move slightly to deflect it, and he darted through the small gap that created and bolted out of the room. The agent turned and fired, and his laughter sounded in their ears. "Missed me."

The agent laughed. "This time. You won't get that lucky again. You, I'm going to kill first."

His Arnold Schwarzenegger impression was impressive. "I'll kill you last."

Diana shook her head. "Okay, so that's how it's gonna be? Fine. From here on out, magic is fair game."

CHAPTER TEN

Ruby followed Diana, her right hand filled with the pistol, her left ready to cast defensive spells as needed. Her partner had explained in the previous moments that the rules of engagement for magical powers were limited to electricity, which the suits could detect and dissipate, and force magic, but only for strikes. She felt somewhat naked without her shield but understood the reasoning behind the training restrictions. She sensed something up ahead and said, "Hold."

Diana stopped, and a moment later replied, "Good catch. Physical trap, hidden with magic. I guess illusion wasn't specifically disallowed."

Ruby laughed. "I kind of thought it was off-limits, but it seems like the other team is playing a little loose with the rules."

"They do that. It opens up possibilities, as well. Let me encase it so that after we move past, we can leave it active in case anyone tries to get us from behind."

They progressed in safety to the next opening. Diana

said, "Illusion isn't my strong suit. Can you make it look like we're entering the room before we actually do?"

"Absolutely. If there's one thing I have a lot of experience with, it's creating illusions." Their doppelgängers materialized over them, forming a sort of double vision for a moment before the apparitions charged into the chamber beyond. Lightning crackled, and automatic gunfire sounded.

Diana ordered, "Go." They ran into the space and found only one enemy. Cara was already moving in the exit's direction when her boss laid down a line of bullets in the way. The other agent skidded to a halt and let her rifle fall, drawing the daggers at her hips and charging at Ruby.

Her partner moved to intervene, but Ruby said, "I've got this."

"You sure?"

She had no time to reply since their foe was already on her. The transparent faceplate revealed a grin on Cara's face as the other woman stepped forward and launched a flurry of attacks. Her daggers stabbed out three times, high, medium, and low, and she finished the sequence with a spinning leg sweep. Ruby blocked the first knife thrust with her pistol, which flew out of her hand at the impact, and the remaining ones with a long force shield in her left hand. She leapt over the foot that tried to steal her legs and snapped out a kick of her own.

The ball of her foot struck her enemy's helmet and pitched her backward. Cara turned the motion into a roll, coming quickly up to her feet and tossing a dagger at Ruby's face. Ruby coated her hand with force magic and slapped the weapon aside, noting in passing that instead of falling, it curved to return to the other woman's grip. "Fancy." She waded in, drawing her sword as she moved and leading with a force blast from her left hand. The other woman raised her dagger, intercepting the magic and grounding it out. Ruby slashed her blade across in a diagonal chop, but Cara stepped aside to avoid the blow.

Ruby's armor stiffened as her foe delivered stabs into her exposed ribs. It made her next kick awkward as she snapped a sidekick into the other woman's stomach that knocked her backward a step. They both moved with a new respect for the other, circling slowly. Cara said, "Nice one. That probably would have put me on the ground in a real fight."

Ruby chuckled. "Assuming I survived the knife wounds, of course."

"You would've had a shield up. Training is a little different. You know," her voice cut off in mid-sentence as she launched her next attack. It was a jumping sidekick that Ruby easily avoided, guiding the other woman's leg off to the side. Cara smashed an elbow back and caught Ruby's helmet. Her faceplate went dark for a moment, apparently simulating a loss of vision, and she reacted by throwing a force wave out in all directions.

When it cleared, her rival was several steps further away, and Diana held a raised pistol pointed at her. Ruby said, "Do it," and the other agent pulled the trigger with a grin. Their opponent went down, and a string of curses that hearkened back to her military background filled the channel. They stood over her locked-up form and smiled down at her.

Diana said, "Aww, did you fall?"

Cara spat another curse and replied, "She's good, but in a real fight, I think I would've won."

Diana shook her head. "In a real fight, it would've been two on one. This wasn't the smartest tactic."

Cara shrugged. "So you say. Still, it was an excellent distraction, don't you agree?"

A canister landed beside her, dropped from above, then detonated. Lightning reached out, locking up Ruby's armor and causing her to fall. Diana hit the floor as well and growled, "Ambush. Stay down, cover the door."

The other woman stiffly climbed to her feet, her training suit simulating significant damage. Ruby reached out with her right hand and used force magic to bring her pistol back to her, then aimed it at the doorway. She summoned a force barrier and put it in front of the opening, ensuring that any enemies would at least have to work to get at them.

That defense solidified not a moment too soon, as Anik leaned around a corner and unloaded a stream from his rifle into the room. The barrage would've surely had one or both of them, but the rounds didn't penetrate her magic. Diana said, "Good job," and drew her sword, transferring the pistol to her left hand. She stepped in front of the opening. "Okay, I'll take over the barrier. You get yourself ready to go." As Ruby obeyed, Diana explained, "I've put a tiny hole in the force shield, only enough of a gap to stick my gun barrel through if someone shows up. There's a small risk, so be sure you stay to my right."

"Seems like it's totally safe. What's the problem?"

The agent shrugged. "Electricity could sneak through and catch me, or fire could penetrate and explode the ammunition in my weapon. Let's not even get started on shadow tentacles."

Ruby carefully didn't touch her forearm and shuddered at the thought. "Yeah, let's not. Those suck."

Once they were as ready as they were going to get, they advanced cautiously, looking for additional traps but finding none. Diana said, "I'm fairly sure we're nearing the end. I know how big the training space is, and it feels like we've covered most of it without doubling back on ourselves. Sometimes the computer sets up a maze, but this map seems to be pretty straightforward. So, probably a safe bet to expect both of our remaining opponents in the next room."

They tried the illusion trick again, but nothing happened as the other figures ran in. Diana muttered, "That's weird. Okay, I'll go in first. You wait five seconds before following." She dashed in, sword and pistol raised, and immediately went down as Anik tackled her. He discharged another of the electricity weapons, taking them both out of the match.

Ruby was already in motion and couldn't stop her charge into the room. She called up a force buckler and looked around carefully for enemies but saw none. Until a laugh sounded from above, where she'd failed to look. She turned in time to see the pair of throwing daggers coming at her face. They struck her helmet, and she was down and out of the fight.

The comm channel went active with all the voices, and the other team crowed and cheered over their leader's loss. Fortunately, Morrigan and Idryll had both gone down before Ruby, so she didn't have to deal with them joining in. Her armor unlocked, and she rose to her feet and traded a fist bump with Rath. "Nice throws, my friend."

He nodded. "Planning to have a training session with Idryll. You can come along."

She grinned. "Absolutely. It's a date."

Diana's voice carried over the others'. "Okay, folks, we'll have a debrief and another run in three hours. In the meantime, grab some lunch, reload, and do whatever else you need to do."

Ruby stepped beside the leader and took off her helmet, gesturing for the other woman to do the same. When she complied, Ruby asked, "Can I have a few minutes to talk to you about something? Something I'd rather no one besides you hears about?"

Diana nodded. "Absolutely. I'll get lunch sent to my quarters. We'll talk there."

CHAPTER ELEVEN

Ruby collapsed into the chair on the visitor's side of Diana's desk. The agent's quarters seemed to have personal space in the back and public space in the front. Diana disappeared momentarily into the former and returned with a pair of towels, rubbing her neck with one and tossing the other to Ruby. The other woman laughed. "Training always works up a sweat. But it's a good sweat. So, lunch should be here in ten minutes or so. What did you want to discuss?"

Now that she was at the moment, Ruby wasn't sure how to start. *Hey, I have a magical artifact stuck in my arm that's babbling at me inside my head about turning me into its meat puppet. How's your day been?* She asked, "Does your sword talk to you?"

Diana rolled her eyes. "Incessantly, and usually at the worst times. No matter how often I tell Fury not to distract me while I'm fighting, those seem to be the moments where unsolicited advice inevitably arrives. I presume you've had a similar experience with yours?"

Ruby nodded. "Yeah. Two voices are inside there, although they're pretty good at not distracting me at bad times." Her words trailed off, and she found no more to replace them.

Diana sat in her chair and leaned backward, putting her feet up on the desk. "I'm not the keenest judge of people, but I sense that asking me about my sword isn't the reason you wanted to have a quiet word. Out with it." The command was playful, but it still felt like an order.

Ruby stood, unfastened the snaps holding the top of her training armor together, pulled her left arm out of its sleeve, and extended it to the other woman. Diana's boots hit the floor as she leaned forward to examine it. "Nice tattoo. I'm guessing it's more than a tattoo, isn't it?" Ruby nodded. "Atlantean artifact?" She nodded again. "Damn, girl. That's some heavy stuff."

Ruby laughed as she got herself properly dressed and sat. "Right? Its voice is becoming a real problem. What do you know about them?"

"Quite a bit, but probably not the things you need to learn. An Atlantean named Rhazdon created most or all of them. Typical power-player, wanted to rule the world or something. Eventually turned out to be not as evil as once thought. That doesn't change the fact that these artifacts are around and still causing trouble after all these years." She shook her head. "We find them and store them away where no one can get at them. It's like putting a single rock in a river's flow for all the good it does. We have a lot of work ahead of us on that score."

"The Mist Elves know virtually nothing about them, so

that's all pretty useful, thanks. You wouldn't happen to know anyone who had one?"

"Not anyone on the side of the angels, anyway. I take it you're finding it a challenge to deal with?"

Sudden tears threatened as a wave of emotion washed over her because someone *understood*, it seemed. She sniffed once to cover it and replied, "Yeah. I need him to shut the hell up, or at the very least, I have to make sure he can't get in my head without my permission. Or something. Basically, I just want him to screw off."

Diana laughed. "It's male?"

Ruby shrugged. "It first appeared as a woman, a Mist Elf ruler, but then turned into an Atlantean man. I guess I have no idea what it really is, if it even has a true state." She managed a crooked smile. "So, any suggestions on how to deal with it?"

The agent rose. "None from me, I'm afraid, but I have a friend who knows just about everything there is to know about, well, everything, I suppose, if you ask her. I'll set up a meeting. You stay here. Lunch should show up shortly. No poking around my bedroom. The magical protections would reduce you to goo."

Ruby's eyes widened. "Really?"

Diana laughed. "No, but keep out anyway. I'll be back in time for the next round of training, and I'll try to get this set up for you as early after that as I can."

After winning the second training scenario, Ruby was tired and satisfied with the knowledge she'd gained as she, Diana, and Rath stepped through the portal to Kemana Stonesreach. It was similar to her home in that it was underground, with a central source of illumination and shops, streets, and houses all around. It was different because the bowl was steeper and the stairs leading upward numerous enough that her legs ached at the sight. Also, instead of the small castle that housed the city's ruler laying in the center, as it did in MountHaven, it was on one end. Diana noticed her looking in that direction. "If you view it from above, it looks vaguely like the sun, with the streets as rays of light shooting out from it. Kind of artistic. Possibly overly aggrandizing."

Ruby laughed. "And the ruler? Ours is an older Mist Elf man."

"This one has a young woman, the Lady. Also an elf. Competent, although I know she irritates Nylotte on a fairly regular basis."

"Is that who we're coming to visit?" The agent had been quiet on the matter. "I've heard her name before, from Shentia."

"Yes. The only advice I can give you is to be honest and don't let her intimidate you. I mean, she will. That's what she does, and it's almost impossible to avoid, but she's not all that. Just *most* of that."

Rath replied, "She's fun."

Diana scowled down at him. "To you, maybe. Try training with her sometime."

The troll shook his head. "No thanks. All good."

Laughter carried them to their destination. Diana opened the door of a nondescript shop, gesturing for Ruby to precede her. She stepped inside and took in the wooden walls, the shelves filled with items that resembled the ones in Shentia's place but more tightly packed, and the white-haired woman sitting primly on a stool behind a counter that lay perpendicular to the door. The Drow said, "Welcome to my place, Ruby Achera. I've heard a great deal about you."

The tone and content of the greeting illustrated the need for Diana's warning against intimidation. Ruby replied, "And I, you. Hopefully what you've heard about me is as positive as what others told me about you."

She didn't answer, merely changed the subject. "Diana. I seem to recall us having a training session scheduled for a couple of days ago."

A sigh came from behind her. "Yes, I sent you a message that I was, uh, *way* out of town that day. We'll get caught up."

The Dark Elf seemed unconvinced, but the corners of her lips turned up as she shifted her gaze to the troll. "Rath, you are a ray of sunshine among these clouds, as always." She gestured at Ruby and Diana to indicate those lacking that illumination. "How are you?"

He jumped up on the counter, and Ruby was positive Nylotte wouldn't have accepted that shocking breach of formality from anyone else on either planet. "Good. Great. I met a tiger-woman. I'm going to teach her to throw knives. She's going to teach me how to fight with claws. Do you have any claws I can use?"

Nylotte laughed. "Indeed, I'm sure there's something around here. Feel free to look." He jumped down with a quiet cheer and started rummaging along the shelves. She turned her attention back to Ruby. "So, Diana said you have a problem that you need help with, but no more than that. Explain."

Ruby could see where Diana's attitude of command came from. She obediently pushed up her sleeve to display the artifact, and the other woman clucked her tongue. "Well, that was a poor decision on your part."

She couldn't stop the scowl from jumping to her face. "Actually, given that I was unconscious at the time after fighting to protect others, it wasn't a choice at all, much less a bad one."

The Drow lifted an eyebrow and shifted her gaze to Diana. "Some fire there."

The agent replied, "Told you."

Nylotte rose. "Very well. Come with me, and we'll talk." She led the way down a staircase to the basement. It was divided roughly into thirds, with a single section nearest the street they'd entered from filled with crates. The other two-thirds combined to create a training space with a polished wooden floor. A trio of rings was inset in the surface, different metals comprising each, decreasing in size from outside to in. The centermost was large enough for the three of them to fit into, but barely. The Dark Elf sat and crossed her legs, gesturing for the others to do the same.

Ruby asked, "What is this space?"

Diana instantly answered, "Torture chamber."

Nylotte laughed. "It's a training room for combat or magic. The rings offer protections, each a different kind. It ensures our conversation will remain private here."

Ruby replied, "Nothing is private from that bastard inside my head."

"Of course, but from everyone else aside from we three, it will be. So, I take it you're looking for ways to deal with your passenger. Diana mentioned you have an artifact sword. Has it been helpful?"

"At times, but it's not enough on its own. I can't go around holding my weapon all the time."

Diana corrected, "Well, you could, but it would look pretty strange."

Nylotte ignored the comment. "Do you have a private space?" Ruby nodded, thinking of the bunker. "Excellent. You should construct rings of your own. With the proper spells, they'll provide a place where you can calm your mind when you need refuge."

"They'll suppress the artifact? For how long?"

The Dark Elf shook her head. "Not exactly. Probably the better metaphor is that they'll give you the high ground in your interactions with it. Plus, when the time comes to fight the artifact for dominance, it will protect you from outside influence."

Ruby replied, "That all sounds great. I can do that."

Nylotte nodded. "Good. Now, let me teach you some basic internal shielding spells you can use to keep it at bay."

Two hours later, when she had finally reached the point of exhaustion from trying to master the techniques Nylotte had taught, Diana and Rath escorted her outside and created a portal to send her back to her kemana. Before she could use it, Diana touched her arm. "What Nylotte didn't say is almost as important as what she did. When the time comes to take on the artifact, be it once or repeatedly, make sure there's someone you trust outside the rings. Should something go wrong, the barriers will protect them from you while they do what needs to be done."

A chill ran through her, and Ruby vowed to herself that she would never let the artifact win. She smiled gratefully. "Got it. Thank you." The agent nodded, and Rath skipped forward for a fist bump.

He said, "You are the law."

Diana laughed and rolled her eyes. "Seriously, Rath, how many times are you going to quote Judge Dredd?"

"Always and forever."

Ruby stepped through and shook her head as the pair started to argue. *Sleep. I need sleep. Then, you artifact bastard, it's time to start putting you in your proper place.* She ignored the dark laughter that came in response.

CHAPTER TWELVE

The exertions of the day before had put Ruby to sleep for more than twelve hours, and she woke refreshed, energetic, and positive. All of that lasted right up until the Atlantean's first chuckle in her mind. She stilled her initial wave of anger and replaced it with the meditative technique Nylotte had taught her, envisioning a glass cube that contained the Atlantean and permitted no sound to escape. That way, he couldn't get up to anything without her seeing it, and he wouldn't influence her.

The walls seemed thin and trembled under his blows, but they held. Both the Drow and Diana had assured her that as her skill in the technique improved, so would the cage's solidity. *Of course, that will last right up until the moment I'm distracted and he smashes through, but at least it's something.* It took another hour to get caffeinated and secure the others' agreement, and she stepped through the portal into the bunker with Idryll behind her, ready to work.

Margrave and Morrigan had both arrived earlier. He

said, "About time we got moving on this place. I expect some return on my investment, you know."

Ruby laughed. "Don't worry. We'll make so many improvements that you won't want to wait to kick us out. But you'll have to."

He put his hands on his hips. "So that's your evil plan? Some way to pay back a friend."

Morrigan interjected, "No, we compensate friends with hard work. Now get to it."

He chuckled, and Ruby pulled him toward the escape tunnel that led to the collapsed building. While they worked on issues involving technology and magic, Morrigan and Idryll were going to do some general cleaning and bring in supplies that weren't atomic-era MREs. Margrave had accused them of being soft for that choice, right up until the moment she offered the old food kits to him. Then his tone changed abruptly, and he started talking about the value of emergency backups.

They reached the end of the passage, and he instructed, "Okay, you push up on the trap door, and I'll catch anything that's up there waiting to fall on us." He produced his wand from out of nowhere like he always did, and she complied. It was a weird sight, seeing the rubble above hovering in place. He didn't seem to be expending significant energy, which impressed her yet again. She hadn't seen him use strong magic before, only very precise power.

Margrave wore a look of concentration as he ordered, "Okay, shift the big stuff out of the way." She complied, and he started stacking smaller pieces into walls around the trap door. After a half-hour's work, he had built a space large enough to stand in, and they both climbed up. Rubble had piled everywhere, but he drew her attention to several areas of structural instability where a solid force blast would clear the path. He gestured toward the walls he'd built. "How good are you with fire?"

She laughed. "I'm the fire *master*."

He snorted. "Okay. Using very precise fire, I want you to heat the edges of the rock so the dust and dirt trapped in between melds to it. Things will shift a little, but I'll keep us from getting crushed, don't worry." She complied again, and the structure seemed more stable when the process was complete. Finally, he withdrew a tube from his cargo pants pocket. "Now, line the joins with this stuff."

As she did so, she asked, "What is it?"

"A proprietary blend of adhesives. This will make sure what you've already put together doesn't break apart."

"Something for the open market?"

He laughed. "One of the reagents is crushed diamond, so probably not."

She whistled. "Pretty serious about this place of yours, huh?"

"Pretty serious about your safety. Someone has to be."

"I have Idryll looking after me. I'm fine."

When the structural work was complete, the next installations were technological. Cameras and sensors guarded all the entrances, plus an internal network with a signal blocker to ensure that signals neither came in nor leaked out. Only one transmission point was permitted, a heavily encrypted broadband connection that would link only to its partner, a module connected to Demetrius's gear. It was part magic, part technology, and, Margrave said, something the military was *very* interested in. Ruby grinned. "I love being the beneficiary of prototyping."

He nodded. "Yeah, it's great, right up until the moment it isn't, and the thing you're testing out blows up on you."

"Dude. Buzzkill."

They added magical wards to the entrances and exits, scratching runes into doorframes to anchor the power. Finally, it was time for what she considered the most important installation. They went to the smallest room, a twelve-by-twelve square that had been an armory but wouldn't be big enough for the three of them to use together. It had been emptied and cleaned meticulously until the wooden walls and concrete floor almost glowed.

Margrave retrieved his toolbox and pulled out a spike attached to a rope, adhering the post magically to the room's center and using the line to draw a perfect circle around it at maximum distance. While he worked, Ruby gazed at the walls. "We should probably put wards in this room, too."

He nodded as he waved his wand at the floor, tracing the line he'd made. "Won't be too hard, but you should do it by yourself. Once I help you get the ring in place, every-thing else here should be yours and yours alone. The others shouldn't even come in."

"Magical purity?"

"Exactly. Make this your place exclusively, and you'll have more power when you're in it."

She cocked her head to the side. "Why do you let people into your workshop, then?"

He paused and lifted an eyebrow. "That's a very smart question. You did learn something at that college of yours."

She snorted, and he continued, "The things I do in the workshop generally don't require that level of purity. When they do, I have another room in my house I can use."

"Really? Why haven't you shown it to me?" He stared at her until she realized what a dumb question that was. "Oh. Yeah. Okay. No anti-college comments. I'm a little distracted these days."

He finished his work and cautioned, "If you don't perfectly focus on this, you could ruin it. Do you want to wait?"

She shook her head. "No, I'm good."

"You're sure?"

"Right as rain. So, force blast to carve out the stone to a depth of six inches, as wide as the channel between the magical barriers you've created."

He nodded. "You shouldn't be able to slip out of line to either side, but you have to be sure to go straight down. My walls will descend to help guide you where I can, but this still requires your skill and focus to ensure it doesn't get misshapen."

Ruby stretched and rolled her neck. "Got it. Let's do this thing."

It took an hour of highly focused work to carve out the channel for the ring, but when they finished, Margrave pronounced it perfect. "Okay, go get the gold." That metal was preferable for the outermost ring because it was highly inert, both chemically and magically. It would effectively ground out any magic that tried to enter or escape. He had procured small bars of the substance, and she slotted them in as he reran the calculations to make sure they had the right amount.

She ran her hands over each before setting it in place, pushing her will into it, her intention for purity and ownership, metaphysical efforts that all the books said were valuable. *Who am I to argue? It only costs me time.* When she was ready, she channeled fire into the metal, hot enough to melt and fuse the ingots. They flowed, then solidified as she used an icy breeze to chill them. When she finished, the ring was solid, seemingly perfect.

Margrave put a hand on her shoulder. "Well done. A definite success. You'll have to do the runes yourself, of course. I can help you make the tool."

She nodded, proud of her effort. "Excellent, but I think that's enough for today. I'm starting to lose focus."

He laughed. "Nope, one more thing. Come with me." They went out to the main room again, where Morrigan and Idryll were snacking on a basket of fruit. Her sister hurled an apple at Ruby, and she snatched it out of the air and took a bite. "Dang, I'm famished, thanks."

Idryll observed, "Next time, throw faster. You almost got her in the head."

Morrigan countered, "You didn't throw at all. What happened, lose your nerve?"

The shapeshifter stopped brushing her arms and scowled. "There's fruit juice in my fur."

They all laughed, and Margrave opened a portal. With another wave of his wand, a small table, slightly wider than it was deep, floated through. It was made of the same stone as the one in his workshop.

Ruby squealed, "For me?" The process of procuring the stone and preparing such a table was intensive, which was why she and Daphne hadn't done it, lacking the time and the resources.

He nodded with a broad smile on his face at the success of his gift. "I think you might need to be alone now and again to relax. Here, away from the outside world, seems like a good place. There's no reason you can't work on your research while you do it. Then it's a double win."

She wrapped him in a hug and bustled off to decide what room to put it in. They all spent the next hour happily in light tasks until the new cell phone that would only work when tied to the bunker's network rang. She answered, and Demetrius's voice came across the line, no hint of flirtation in it. "There's a recording in the email account. Alejo is trying to get hold of you. I didn't listen beyond the first second, but her tone sounds serious."

CHAPTER THIRTEEN

The message from Alejo had been short and sweet. "Need to meet." Their arrangement meant it was on Ruby to choose the time and place since that was the safest option for her. *One never knows when the PDA is watching, and those bastards have hardly any scruples at all.*

She suited up in her full uniform, draped herself in a veil, and portaled to the sheriff's backyard. She called to ask the woman to come outside, waiting on the swing as she had before.

Sheriff Valentina Alejo didn't offer her a bottle this time, knowing she wouldn't remove her mask to drink it, and sipped her beer before speaking. The moonlight left her face shadowy. "The head of the local PDA reached out. They want to meet with you. Well, you and your friends."

"Seriously? And they figured you could put that together for them how?"

She shrugged. "Our paths have crossed a number of times. I suppose it's not unreasonable."

"A call won't suffice?"

Alejo laughed, low and dismissive. "It wasn't offered as an option. It may be that they don't just want to exchange words, if you know what I mean. Seems like a classic setup, doesn't it?"

Ruby nodded. "It does. Who specifically?"

"Guy from the Reno office who's been nosing around town for a while. I got the impression this is his new home, temporarily at least."

She scowled. "Think he's trying to make a name for himself? Pushing the boundaries a bit, taking advantage of the situation? There's certainly a lot more PDA presence in town now than ever before."

Alejo nodded. "Maybe, although my understanding is that PDA offices have significant operational latitude in the first place. For all I know, this could be standard operating procedure. My concern is that if this meeting doesn't happen, they might start putting pressure on my office, either to use us or to cut us out of whatever's going on."

Ruby sighed. "Well, SOP or not, I'm definitely not bringing the others along if I decide to talk to them. That would be like offering ourselves up on a silver platter. If I didn't do it for that scumbag Sloane, I'm certainly not planning to do it for the paranoid defense agency."

The joke earned a chuckle. "Seems like a smart move."

Ruby asked, "Do you think this is important, in the big picture?"

The other woman nodded. "Selfishly, I don't want them messing with my people because they can't get to you. Overall, they're clearly planning to be here for the long term. You'll have to deal with them anyway, so might as well get it done."

"Okay. Set up a meet at the Casino Graveyard. Midnight tomorrow. He has to be there in person for me to show up."

Alejo laughed. "Do you want me to tell him to come alone and unarmed, too?"

Ruby let out a soft snort. "No, I'm not that stupid. But make it clear that if he's not there, I won't be either."

Ruby had set the meeting for the next day rather than rousting the agent out of bed for an immediate chat because preparations were required. By the time midnight rolled around, she had improved the drones Demetrius had bought for her, outfitting one of them with a special tool she'd crafted and all three with the concealment magic tech she'd been working on. She was confident the PDA versions wouldn't be able to see through it. *Especially if they have no idea such a thing exists, right?*

She paced behind Demetrius's computer chair, his bedroom offering precious little space in which to burn off her nervous energy. The infomancer had connected to all three drones, which she'd concealed near the meeting site earlier in the day so they wouldn't have to waste battery power flying to get there. Each had a small solar panel on the top that would have topped off their batteries as they waited in the camouflaged spots she'd left them. *I don't think I could've prepared for this any better. Now hopefully the PDA shows up on time.*

She didn't doubt that the PDA agent would bring friends. He'd be stupid not to, especially since he had to figure she'd chosen the location for a reason. *Even if I had shown up in person, it would've been reasonably easy to escape from there. Maybe he does just want to talk. Guess we'll see.* With twenty minutes to go, Demetrius brought the drones out from cover, sending one up high to surveil the site. At one minute before the appointed time, a trio of black SUVs pulled in and formed a triangle around the clearing she'd selected for their meeting. A government sedan followed them, probably one of the bulletproof glass models, and agent Paul Andrews emerged from it. *You slimy bugger.*

Margrave had dropped off a speaker at the site for her earlier in the day, under a veil and in disguise, in case they were watching. She activated the connection. "What can I do for the Paranormal Defense Agency?" The drone caught the echoes as her voice bounced around the clearing, and every one of the agents turned in a circle, drawing weapons and looking for her. The agent in charge shook his head. "Games? Really?"

The screens in front of her displayed feeds from all three drones. One hovered over the vehicles, high enough that they shouldn't be able to hear the fans, giving her a big picture look at what was going on. The second one was still in its concealed location, waiting for circumstances to call it into play. The third, one of the tiny versions she'd built to take into the field, moved smoothly along a path they'd scouted out beforehand, just far enough off the ground that it wouldn't reveal itself by disturbing the dust and dirt.

She replied, "You must think I'm either stupid or ridiculously trusting to show up with all *my* people where all *your* people could get at us. I'm a lot of things, but *that* naïve, I'm not."

He put his hands on his hips. "Yet, here I am, as you asked me to be. You're not holding up your end of the bargain."

She laughed, enjoying the fact that he had no idea he'd been in a room with her before, had her literally at arm's length. The microphone distorted her voice, rendering it unrecognizable. The speaker had a small charge to destroy it when they finished, so there'd be no way to trace that back to her, either. "Oh, please, Agent Andrews. Let's be professionals. I needed to see how you'd act. It was a predictable response, fortunately, so we can probably talk."

He crossed his arms. "Fine. I'll be brief. You need to stop what you're doing and let us handle things."

"You've been doing such a good job so far. I think the owners of the Mist would totally agree." She slapped Demetrius on the shoulder, having no desire to continue the conversation any longer than necessary.

He muted the microphone and said, "Shush. This is harder than it looks."

"I thought you were supposed to be awesome at this stuff. Put me back on." He activated the mic, and she added, "Let's say for the sake of argument that I trusted you to take care of things. What would happen to my friends and me?"

He shrugged. "The usual. Debriefings, release."

Ruby laughed. "Yeah, right." On the screen in front of her, the drone was finally close enough to fire its payload. A tracking device flew out and stuck onto the back of the car, the small black magnetic pearl more or less invisible against the vehicle's skin. "Anyway, while it's been nice chatting, I have to go. Here's the plan: you stay out of my way, and I'll stay out of your way. We'll both be happy. Otherwise, things could go badly, and you'll wind up on the losing end of that particular tally."

She pointed, and Demetrius hit the button to activate the charge inside the speaker, destroying it. On the video feed, the agents reacted, spinning toward the noise, then piled back into their cars and drove away. The small drone returned to its concealed location for pickup later, and the one up high kept track of the vehicles under Demetrius's guidance. The third, set to follow the tracking device automatically, rose into the air and started moving. Ruby clapped Demetrius on the shoulder. "Great work, Tree. Now I need to get ready to go have a real conversation with that douchebag."

He nodded. "Remember, you owe me another date."

She laughed, rolled her eyes, and gave him a lingering kiss on the neck. "Yeah, yeah, whatever. You'd be so bored without me."

She left the room before he could argue, headed for her one-on-one with Agent Andrews.

CHAPTER FOURTEEN

The drone tracked the locator back to a home in a residential area to the southeast of the Strip. Ruby portaled as close as she could, then used an autonomous vehicle to take her the rest of the way. She rode in the disguise of an elderly human man in a tracksuit, in case anyone happened to be looking for her. With a couple of blocks to go, she bailed out and traveled toward the agent's house through several backyards. The drone hovered overhead, providing a view of the home, and before she entered its range she muttered, "I'm here," into her comm.

A click of acknowledgment sounded, and she crept into the fenced-in area at the rear of the agent's home. Her magical senses were on the lookout for traps, and her eyepieces cycled through detection modes to help her spot mundane ones. She launched her other drone, this one controlled by the small phone-like device Margrave had created, and piloted it close to peer into the home's windows.

The first floor showed a kitchen and a living room-dining room combination area. The second contained a home office and two bedrooms with an apparently sleeping Paranormal Defense Agency boss-type person occupying one. She asked, "Tree, any security system inside?"

He replied, "Activate the booster." She reached down to her belt and hit the switch on the device that would allow him faster access to the area's computer networks. After thirty seconds or so, he said, "Okay, I'm into it. I set it into maintenance mode. It will still register what goes on but won't trigger any alarms or call out."

"You're the best."

"Now you owe me even more. I'm thinking a weekend away, with you focused entirely on pampering me."

"Yeah, yeah, put it on my to-do list." She used force magic to release the latch on the window, then tried to slide it open. It didn't move, and she brought the drone around for a better look. The image it sent back showed a wooden board wedged into place to prevent the pane from rising. *Old school, simple and smart. You might not be the total idiot I took you for. Also, I need to cut those for all the windows and sliding doors in our house.*

Concentrating carefully, she used magic with one hand to move the wood out of the way and the other to lift the window. The wooden rectangle fell to the grass. Ruby reestablished her veil, force-blasted herself up to the second floor, and clambered up to sit on the windowsill with a leg on either side. She drew a breath to speak.

The figure on the bed twitched. Suddenly, a gun whipped around to point at her. She knocked it from his hand with force magic and waggled a finger after letting her veil fall. "Now, now. Be nice. I thought you wanted to talk."

He sat up, offering her a view of his bare chest, the chiseled nature of which suggested he put in significant time at the gym. *Unfortunately, no amount of pumping iron can compensate for being a scumbag.* He replied, "Yeah, this wasn't quite what I had in mind."

She grinned and hoped her dragon's face scared him a little. "Well, that's not my problem. You didn't really think I'd bring my friends along and expose them to whatever nonsense you had planned, did you? What do you want?"

"Can I get up?"

"No."

"Okay, can I grab a shirt then?"

She shook her head. "Also no. Talk."

He sighed and ran his hands through his rumpled brown hair. "I'll be direct. There's no place for vigilantes in this town anymore. We're here now, and we have it all in hand. You and your friends need to step down."

She barked a laugh. "Yeah, but that would require someone *useful* to step up. I don't really dig your methods, what with the heavy-handed tactics and the constant surveillance. What's next, random searches of people on the Strip?"

He shrugged. "Gotta do what you gotta do to keep the innocent safe."

"See, on that we agree. I have to do the same."

Agent Andrews grinned suddenly for no apparent reason. "So, no way I can convince you to give it up and come in peacefully? Or, failing that, to fade away into the night, so I don't have to worry about you and your buddies causing trouble?"

Ruby scowled. "Causing trouble? Have you been paying attention at all?"

The receiver in her ear *pinged* softly. Demetrius advised, "Agents moving in. Looks like they've established an outer perimeter about two blocks around and are pushing forward. Lots of them."

The half-naked man in the bed started to speak, and she cut him off. "Yeah, I know, you're trying to keep me here while your friends move in for the kill. You couldn't play nice, just once? That's too bad."

She called up a force shield with one hand, placing it between him and the nightstand beside him, then used the other to blast the piece of furniture to shards. The barrier prevented any of them from striking him, but the demonstration of the instant conversion from functional object to kindling inspired a look of shock on his face. Ruby nodded. "You might wish to consider if us being on different sides is *really* what you want."

He threw himself off the far side of the bed, his hand reaching for something on that side's nightstand, and she fell backward out of the window. She landed on a soft burst of magic, cast a veil, and snuck away. After a minute of careful creeping, she encountered one of the oncoming agents and angled to avoid him, making sure her sound and sight concealment was at full strength.

Her magic failed with a whisper of strangeness, and he spotted her. He shouted, whipped his gun around, and pulled the trigger. She dove to the ground and rolled to elude the stream of bullets, cursing under her breath. "What the hell?"

Morrigan replied, "They have weird backpacks on. Maybe they're the same things that the bastard on the Strip had? Some sort of portable anti-magic emitter?"

Ruby cursed again. "Okay, give them points for coming prepared, anyway. Fortunately, I also brought my backup people, who are way better than Paul Andrews'. Let's mix it up."

A low crunching emanated from the trees behind the man, and Idryll slammed into him, knocking him forward onto his face. The tiger-woman dropped to one knee and delivered a punch to his head that caused a *crack* to echo through the area. She said, "Just the nose, I think. He should be out for a while. Do you want the backpack?"

Ruby did, but getting it like this was too dangerous. "No. There could be tracking devices or any number of other surprises. Plus, we truly have to get out of here before fate gives them a break, and we don't need the extra weight. Tree, I could use a clear vector."

His voice carried unexpected concern. "There really isn't one. The agents are closing in from everywhere, and more are arriving. I don't think it's their entire complement or anything, but there are a *lot* of the bastards. They called for backup from local PD, too. They'll be on-site in ten minutes or so."

Ruby replied, "Okay. We're going to break through to the south, then. As soon as we're out of the range of these stupid things, we'll portal out of here." *Which is what I should've done in the first place, but I was being clever. Or paranoid. Or both.* She needed to solve her portaling problem.

"Morrigan, if you're clear to portal, you should get out of here."

"The hell I will." A cacophonous mix of light and sound came from the north as Morrigan either fired one of her flash-bang arrows or used one of Margrave's grenades.

Ruby frowned. "Are you on top of the agent's house?"

Her sister laughed. "Maybe. Following you now. Go."

She and Idryll moved on parallel tracks, hunting for PDA personnel. The tiger-woman took them out quietly, one after the next, her natural skills much better than Ruby's in the absence of magic. They finally came up against the outer perimeter, created by groups of four at thirty-foot or so intervals. She breathed, "Damn, they're pretty serious about this whole thing."

Morrigan stepped up behind her. "Well, you do have a rare talent for upsetting people."

Idryll muttered, "She's right, you do."

Ruby shook her head. "Gas them, and we'll hit whoever doesn't fall." An arrow sailed above with a slight *whir*, landing in the center of the quartet. Billows of vapor came out, and one of them fell instantly. The other three quickly brought masks to their faces, and in that moment of distraction, Ruby and Idryll struck. Ruby raced forward and led with her left, punching the nearest agent's ribs. When he tried to bring his rifle around to point at her, she whipped a right cross over it, connecting with his cheek. The stun knuckles detonated, knocking him unconscious. She used the momentum from the blow to twist herself into a spin and smash an elbow into the face of the next closest foe. He got the butt of his rifle up in time to deflect it a little, preventing it from being a knockout shot.

Ruby did another half-turn and whipped her leg around in a roundhouse kick that slammed into his thighs, the strike to the nerve junction numbing his nearer limb. He went down on one knee, and she punched down with her right, discharging another shock blast. She turned to see that Idryll had unsheathed her claws, and the other woman had cut the rifle away from the man, along with the backpack he wore. She grabbed the back of his head with her left hand and brought it down to meet her rising left knee, and the man fell backward with a groan. Her partner lifted the bag. "Sure you don't want this?"

"No, same reasons as before. Let's get out of here."

Idryll dropped the object with a shake of her head. "Missed opportunity."

Morrigan sauntered up and observed, "Yeah, a missed chance to get caught. You know they're going to have a locator on that thing."

The trio continued to bicker over their comms as they took out more PDA personnel drawn by the fight's noise, disabled all the emitters, and hastily portaled away as soon as they had a slim opening with working magic.

CHAPTER FIFTEEN

Julianna Sloane was impressed with her subordinates. That wasn't an unfamiliar situation, but in this case, Smith had outdone himself. It had only taken him a matter of days to secure and furnish a luxurious apartment high in a tower overlooking the Vegas Strip and arrange the move from Reno to Vegas. She stood before the wall of windows in her bedroom and gazed down at the early morning pedestrians as sunrise broke over the horizon. *This is right. This is what I need.*

A glance at the expensive watch gracing her wrist, a gift from her late husband, told her it was time to go. She arrived in the living room at the same moment as Vicki Thompson. The other woman had added a chunky silver necklace to her outfit of black turtleneck and pinstripe suit, and it suited her perfectly. It looked heavy enough to be wrapped around the knuckles as a weapon or unsnapped and used as a short-range whip.

Julianna's husband had taught her the ins and outs of such things, training her to keep a wary eye on her surroundings in a way that she never had before. Her sense of potential dangers had been relatively refined to begin with, but it became far better developed after Gabriel's instruction. She shook her head, pushing away sad thoughts, and smiled at Thompson. "Are we good to go?"

She nodded. "Yes. They're assembled, having coffee and donuts."

Julianna chuckled. "Just like a corporate meeting, right? Well, it's an unusual kind of corporation, but the concepts are similar enough, I suppose. Let's go." Her security had recommended she no longer have visitors in her apartment, and in any case, she wouldn't have wanted these particular people in her private domain. They entered the boardroom after a short elevator ride, and she nodded at the assembled group. They were a fairly hard-looking bunch, and despite their quasi-professional dress, their violent backgrounds were apparent, be they military, martial arts, or simply life experience.

The space held a mix of men and women, several races, and multiple species. While Julianna had a problem with the Oriceran immigrants in Magic City, she had no particular feelings one way or the other toward magicals in general. They were merely people, all of them with similar vices, similar desires, and varying levels of aptitude to achieve them. *Hopefully, they'll manage better than last time. Fifty percent simply won't do.*

She smiled and took the seat at the head of the table, smoothing her trousers before she sat. Skirts and dresses were a thing of the past until she was well and truly over Gabriel's loss, which seemed appropriate given how much he appreciated her in them. "Thank you for coming today. I have a proposition for you all."

A large, dark-skinned man with a bald head and a thick mustache occupied the closest chair on her left. He smoothly inserted, "Seems like a lot of top-end talent here. You wouldn't be putting us in competition with one another, would you?" He cracked his knuckles. "Not that I'm against that. It should simply be something we know from the outset."

Others around the table made jokes or tossed insults his way, suggesting that the community of professional bounty hunters was reasonably close. *Well, professional* extralegal *bounty hunters, I guess. Certainly there are no James Brown-stones among this group.*

She widened her smile. "Honestly, I don't care how the job gets done, as long as it gets done. My preference would be that you each decide upon an individual target and go after them. If you fail, that target can be available to others to pick up once they've accomplished their tasks. Truly, the mechanisms by which this all gets taken care of don't matter to me in the least. What matters is success, in a rapid timeframe."

Another one opened their mouth as if they would ask a question, and Julianna raised her hand and said, "Allow me to finish, as I believe many of your queries will be addressed by what I have to say. All of you are aware, I'm sure, that Gabriel Sloane was my husband. Doubtless you also know how he made his name and what he attempted most recently." Nods answered her. "That project wasn't completed. *That* is a problem I intend to rectify. Simply put, I'm declaring war on the casino owners in Magic City and won't embrace peace until I have what I want."

The same man who'd spoken before did so again. "What is that, exactly?"

She gave a slight shake of her head. "Overall strategy and goals rest with me exclusively. What you need to know are the tasks I have for you. Simply put, the casino owners need to hurt. Punishment will bring them to the negotiating table faster than any other route. However, challenges exist."

A Drow woman in black leather laughed. Her hair was buzzed short, a look Julianna had never seen on one of the Dark Elves, and gave her a vicious first impression. "They'll have lots of security, no doubt. That will make planning vital. And expensive."

She waved that thought away. "Rest assured that I have the resources to cover any reasonable expenses. Just clear them with my people, first." She gestured toward Smith and Thompson, who stood to the side of the room. "They will be your contacts going forward for all things related to this project. Before you leave here today, they'll collaborate with you to identify targets and assist in setting budgets."

Another person at the table, a heavily muscled man in a leather jacket that seemed to be straining to contain his bulk, asked, "How do we know you're good for it?"

She responded to that question with a thin smile. "I'm not exactly going to open my books to you all if that's what you mean. However, you'll each receive twenty-five thousand dollars as compensation for taking this meeting. I'll reimburse approved expenses within a day. For those who accomplish their tasks, hospitalizations will be paid at one rate and deaths at another. The big prize, the goal you should aim for, is to take your target alive. I'll pay the most for anyone who gives me the leverage I need to achieve my goals."

The Drow nodded. "As a logical extension of that thought, parents would be most effectively compromised if we take their children."

Julianna shrugged. "I agree, that's the way I see it, but I entrust those details to you and my lieutenants. But, one can't go wrong with the tried-and-true methods, right?" The table broke into laughter, and she rose. "I'll leave you to it. Any questions, work through them. Thank you in advance. This will be a lucrative arrangement for all of us, and I look forward to having you on my side."

Several hours later, Thompson and Smith joined her in the apartment's living room. She'd ordered lunch from the restaurant downstairs and had a tray of sandwiches, another of desserts, and beverage options galore in the kitchen's drink cooler. She had popped the cork on a bottle of champagne and offered the others a glass for a toast. "To Gabriel Sloane. May his vision be realized."

They replied, "To Gabriel," and they all drank. After her lieutenants had made their food and beverage choices, she asked, "So, how did it go?"

Thompson said, "I think a couple aren't big-league enough for this project. They'll take their money and go."

Julianna ventured, "The large one in the jacket?"

Smith laughed. "You have great insight into people,

boss. Yeah, we agree. That one isn't up to something at this level. Most of the others are, though."

"Any of them quail at the idea of kidnapping the kids?"

Thompson nodded. "Not out loud, of course, but you could see it in their faces when we discussed it. We assigned those targets without children, plenty of principals to send them after."

"Good decision. Make sure you have planned intervals to reassess our strategy. Things may change depending on who is successful and who isn't."

Smith replied, "That's already in the plan. They have three days to execute on the initial round. Then we take stock of the situation."

Juliana frowned. "I wish they could do it today." Energy surged inside her, a mix of anger and anticipation. "Those bastards are going to learn the hard way that they should've agreed in the first place." Her subordinates nodded. "I guess I better get moving on some of my work related to the aftermath. Oh, I almost forgot. Speaking of deadlines, what's the status of our security company in Ely?"

Smith chuckled. "You definitely lit a fire under them. There's a new magical-only outfit in town, and apparently, the newcomers soundly rejected their overtures to partner up or buy them out. Word is, they'll be taking them out within the same timeframe as our other operations."

Juliana grinned. "Excellent. And a backup has been identified in case they fail?"

Thompson nodded. "Two. One we can persuade with money, the other might require a little strong-arming."

"I'm lucky to have the both of you. Keep me apprised.

Now, while we eat, tell me a bit about yourselves. Honestly, for as long as you've worked for me, I feel like I hardly know you. While that might've been how my husband preferred it, here in Vegas it's time for a new beginning. So, who wants to go first?"

CHAPTER SIXTEEN

Grentham looked around at his subordinates with a measure of concern. While they were adequate to the tasks he usually set them in the black market trade in magical items, he hadn't chosen them for martial prowess. *Circumstances being what they are, I guess I have no choice.* He maintained an outward appearance of confidence, giving them a serious expression tinted with the hint of a smile. "Okay, people. New wrinkle in our ongoing adventures. We've been contracted to assist a local security company in an operation tonight."

One of the dwarves who had been with him longest chimed in, "That wouldn't be your security company, would it?"

Grentham chuckled. "It would, indeed. I know this is a little outside our norm, but you'll get a bonus payment and a share of whatever we take from them. Of course, my partner and I will have first choice."

Nods and mutters of assent followed. That was always

the deal. The ones at the top chose their rewards. Then the others got the rest based on position. It kept them interested in climbing through the ranks. He tossed a small black canvas bag to the nearest man. "Take one and pass it along. You need to put these buttons on underneath your clothes, where the opposition won't notice them." A couple of his people looked dubious, and he shrugged. "If you'd like to get shot by your side, ignore or lose the button. If that doesn't sound fun, make sure it stays close."

The bag moved faster after that, and they made a show of securing the items. He nodded approval. "There will be rifles for those who want them. Otherwise, choose your own weapons carefully. We'll meet at the appointed location in ninety minutes. Any problems, call me. If anything changes, I'll call you."

He retreated into his office and closed the door, then portaled to his *other* office in the Aces Security building. He arrived in the locker room in time to hear the end of Jared's speech giving their usual operatives and employees the same instructions. The plan was to mix the groups, with one of their regulars in charge of several of his magicals, and he and Jared each leading half of the total force.

He plopped the box he'd brought along onto the table in the center of the room. "Everyone load up with at least one magazine of anti-magic bullets. The likelihood that we'll wind up shooting at humans is really low, so these should make everything better and hopefully not break the bank. Remember not to shoot my people. Your goggles should display them as friendlies, but if in doubt, take a second to check."

One of their longest-serving personnel, a woman with a blonde flat-top haircut that looked perfectly bristly, gave a short laugh. "They're not going to shoot us, are they?"

Grentham grinned. "You're in charge, so I guess that depends on your behavior." Laughter bounced around the space, and he shook his head. "Seriously, I've warned them that we'll be facing magical opposition, most likely, so you should be fine. They're good people. Just keep them under tighter control than you might this bunch of reprobates." He gestured at the others in the room and got a few theatrical scowls and one obscene gesture. "Great. Call us if you need anything. We're going to go do our prep."

He and Jared visited the lobby to ensure their surveillance folks were on the case, even though they'd be playing a backup role in that night's operation. The main terminal was manned by their best, and several others worked at laptops around the room to help coordinate communication. He said, "Looks good to me."

His partner nodded. "Me too. We can check this box on the to-do list." They moved deeper into the building, home to their secure armory. Grentham was going with body armor for the operation, not his normal choice, since he respected the other company and wasn't sure what tricks and traps they might have waiting for invaders. Jared made the same selection. Vests, helmets with transparent face-plates, fatigues underneath, and steel-toed boots wrapped them in protection.

Grentham selected a shotgun filled with slugs instead of buckshot, planning to use it as a lock breaker if needed. Otherwise, he'd rely on his magic. Jared took a shotgun as well, but also a rifle and a pair of pistols. Truth be told, if he hadn't had his magic to depend upon, Grentham would've opted for a howitzer if he could figure out a way to carry it. He observed, "This won't be easy."

His partner shook his head. "No. I'm not sure what we'll find, but these folks are serious players, so we have to assume they'll be ready for this. Still, our people are good, and we have a lot of them. Speaking of which, are we all set with Scimitar?"

Grentham nodded and bent to unzip a satchel he'd brought along. "We are. They couriered these to me about an hour ago." He handed over a black box, about as large as his hand and three times as thick. It had standard straps to attach to their equipment belts.

Jared asked, "Network extender?"

"That's what I'm told. I have no reason to doubt."

His partner looked dubiously down at the device. "You know, this would be a great way to carry out an assassination. Get the targets to put the bombs on themselves, then boom."

Grentham laughed. "Don't go paranoid on me, buddy. Besides, I took them through our explosives detector already."

"Good to know that we're both still on the ball." Jared visibly adjusted his attitude with a squaring of his shoulders and a deep breath. "Okay, are we forgetting anything?"

Grentham patted his thigh pouches to ensure his potion flasks were inside. As long as he had those, there wasn't much else to worry about. "The vans?"

Jared replied, "They'll be where we planned.

Autonomous. You're positive your infomancer can hack them?"

"They said so. Our people downstairs have the explosives?"

He nodded. "All set. Enough to make sure no one gets any evidence out of them when we finish."

"You have your healing pack?" They had access to some of the latest military tech, and an AI-controlled trauma kit was the best of the bunch.

His partner patted his thigh pouch. "Right here. Let's hope like hell we don't have to use it." That was an extra sincere statement since the only one who would use it would be Jared himself. *We all need a failsafe.*

Grentham clapped his hands together. "Okay, I think we're set. The only thing we haven't talked about is ground rules. I assume there are none?"

Jared laughed. "After the reception they gave us, I can't imagine taking out the leadership will shift the others to our cause. Everyone we see goes down."

"Agreed. And we get as much of their gear out of there as we can."

"You've secured a neutral location to check it over?" They were both highly cognizant of the possibility that the security company would have trackers on their most valuable equipment, similar to the ones they used.

"Yeah, a warehouse way to the south. The infomancer set it up. Not traceable back to us. I can make a portal to transfer stuff over."

Jared frowned. "Can anyone else, if you're, say, indisposed?"

Grentham laughed. "Nope, only me. So you better make sure I stay alive."

He shrugged. "I'll handle my end of the operation. More than that, I cannot do."

"That'll be sufficient." He opened his thigh pouch to double-check that the potions were there, even though he *knew* they were because he'd just felt them. *Getting paranoid in your old age. Then again, there's no other way to reach old age, not in this world.* "All right. Let's hit the vans and get the proverbial show on the literal road."

Grentham bailed out of the van a half-mile away from the guard post that controlled access to the complex. They could have entered on foot, but the likelihood of surveillance was too high, and he wasn't confident his people could remain magically concealed against whatever detection their targets might have in place.

Instead, they'd ride in fast and hard in the vans, then execute a rapid deployment that would hopefully take the building's defenders by surprise. Their drones flew high overhead, and a summary of what they saw flowed into his earpiece in a constant stream. Overall, it was a lot of noise and precious little information. He shook his head and focused on covering the ground to the guard post.

When it was a short distance away, he said, "Everyone, go." While he'd been closing, the vans would've been loading up his people at the rally point and moving into position for the run to their target. As soon as he received acknowledgment that they were rolling, he covered himself in a veil and rushed toward the single guard gazing alertly over the road leading to his domain.

He considered using the axes on his belt, his tried-and-true weapons of choice, but saw no particular reason for the hireling to die. The man wasn't part of the group they were taking on, only a guy doing a job for probably too little money. He stepped inside, let his veil fall, and blasted the man with lightning. The guard fell to the floor, and Grentham pulled the zip ties from the man's belt and bound him. He hit the button to open the gate as the vans came into view. The rearmost paused long enough for him to jump on board, then sped quickly ahead.

Jared announced, "Fifteen seconds to target. Van one to the right, vans two and three center, van four left."

The infomancer's computer-modulated voice said, "I've acquired their network signal. Beginning intrusion."

Ideally, their cyber warrior would get the doors open for them. If not, Grentham had the shotgun. If that proved insufficient, and his magic couldn't do it either, well, there was more than one reason they'd brought along so many explosives. *Never hurts to have a little extra boom in reserve.*

The vans screeched to almost simultaneous halts, and they piled out. Jared was already marching toward the door with a shotgun out when Grentham got himself moving. Scimitar said, "Come on in," and the lobby entrance opened.

He replied, "Nice work. Internal defenses?"

"Still active. There's at least one live infomancer resisting me, plus an AI. Might be more of each, can't tell yet. Assume everything except the external alarm is alive. I have that locked down." She'd explained ahead of time that she planned to send in a signal-jamming drone and was confident she could block the hardline if one existed.

A chime that indicated a private channel between him and Jared opening sounded, and his partner said, "We're depending on Scimitar more than I'd like."

Grentham shrugged. "Get it done fast and we won't have to worry about it. You head in. I'll secure the lobby and follow as soon as I can."

Jared's teams included three subordinates, each in charge of five of Grentham's magicals. He was glad to have them along but didn't have any real trust in them. If blood spilled on their side, he'd do his best to make sure it wasn't their regular people. He detailed one group to move ahead, with his most reliable lieutenant, Claire Kendris, and Karna, the dwarf his partner had identified as the most proficient at sensing magic.

They made it only ten feet down the corridor toward the conference room, near the first intersection, when both of them barked, "Hold." His subordinate continued, "Got a laser eye."

Jared tapped the button on the side of his goggles that would display electrical emanations, looking all around to see what the detection device connected to. Nothing showed. "Whatever it feeds must be powered down. Can you disengage it?"

"We have the technology, boss. Thirty seconds."

"Okay, what do we have on the magical side?"

The dwarf replied, "Can't tell for sure. Doesn't feel like

a cloak. Maybe a backup sensor, in case we spot the laser. Seems to be at floor level." He had descended to one knee and held a hand parallel to the ground, about a foot up.

Jared frowned. "Can you get us past it?"

"Send Chan up." Another of Grentham's people advanced, and the pair chatted briefly. Then, Chan waved his arms, and Karna said, "There will be a step up here." If he tilted his head just right, Jared could see the shimmer that indicated a layer of force now resting over the carpet.

Kendris reported, "We're good."

Jared nodded. "Okay, Team Two, you branch off to the left. Keep an eye out for traps. My team and Team Three will continue forward." His second most trusted lieutenant was in charge of Team Two. Arguably, that should've been reversed, with his most reliable operative heading up the other team. However, his prime goal was to survive the encounter and he'd shift anything he needed to increase the probability of that happening. When Team Three was halfway across the force barrier, it suddenly vanished, and they dropped to the floor, requiring them to take a moment to catch their balance. He barked, "What happened?"

The infomancer replied, "Anti-magic emitters came to life all around the place. I'd say their defensive posture has switched from passive to active."

Jared frowned. "Well, *hell*."

Grentham said, "Unexpected, but we can deal with it. Most of my people took rifles, so we still have solid offensive capability. Scimitar, are you able to identify the emitters?"

"Working on it."

Jared asked, "What are you thinking?"

"By activating the emitters, they've eliminated the ability to portal in reinforcements. If we can selectively activate or deactivate them, that whole defense will work to our advantage."

The computer modulated voice said, "Yes, on identifying them. I can probably turn them off at will although how long I'll be able to keep them that way is anyone's guess. Plus, there's always the possibility that they can do the same, so you should be wary of sudden magical attacks."

Jared replied, "Got it. Moving forward."

Grentham thought for a second, then decided to switch up his strategy a little. "Let's do this. Turn off whatever emitters cover the lobby in three minutes. We'll give them a landing point and see if they'll take the bait." He moved two of his teams that were originally supposed to follow Jared to help explore the building and positioned them around the lobby with their backs against the walls and weapons pointing more or less toward the center, careful to avoid crossfire.

He patted the senior-most Aces Security personnel on the shoulder. "I'm taking one team inside. You hold here. If anyone shows up, whoever they are, you burn them down." The man nodded, and Grentham clarified. "Well, anyone other than the police, or the sheriff, or the PDA, that is. If those folks show, yell a warning and portal away." They had very few limits on the night's operation, but getting themselves branded outlaws was not on the list of acceptable outcomes.

He reviewed the positioning of his people and decided it was the best he was going to get. He toggled his microphone on. "Okay, I'm on the move. Keep pushing forward, and we'll meet you in the back."

CHAPTER SEVENTEEN

Jared and his team navigated several more technological traps, and by the time they'd reached the third, the info-mancer had achieved a deep enough access to display what they were attached to. When he saw, Jared exclaimed, "Holy hell, they're not messing around." If they inadvertently triggered one of the traps, a ceiling turret would have descended to hose down the trapped area with bullets. In the absence of magic caused by the emitters, the assault would be equally lethal to anyone in range.

Thus far they'd encountered laser eyes, motion detectors, and a heat sensor, solutions for which they'd prepared in advance. They were only thirty seconds off the planned timetable, which was a total win, in his opinion. The building was full of offices, as expected, but most of them turned out to be unoccupied at the moment and appeared as if they went unused during the day, as well. Jared said, "This is ridiculous. There have to be defenders here, right? Or is this some sort of elaborate trap?" With each step deeper into the facility, his nervousness about the situation grew.

Grentham replied, "I guess, given the ability to portal, they could use this building as a front but operate out of their main base. That's not that bad an idea."

Scimitar's voice came over the line. "An anti-magic emitter just switched off in the section beyond the one you're in, Team One. Be wary."

Jared said, "Acknowledged. Weapons ready, people. Magicals right behind our trap detectors, shields up as soon as you have the ability." He always pictured magical shields acting like the ones in *Star Trek*. *That's just what the Enterprise needed, a wizard or two.*

Their path led them into the building's huge garage, which occupied probably half of the facility's square footage on the first couple of floors. It had appeared as simply a big open space on the blueprints, but the external doors the recon drone had spotted gave away its purpose. What was entirely unexpected was the complete lack of vehicles and the presence of the welcoming committee, led by the elf they'd met earlier, all of them holding riot shields. She waved. "Fancy meeting you again, Mr. Trenton."

He nodded. "We did explain there would be consequences for not joining us."

She laughed. "Consequences for *you*, I'd say."

Grentham advised, "We're coming your way as fast as we can. Stall her."

Jared clasped his hands behind his back. "There's still time to change your mind. We could turn this into a party, knock down a few drinks together, discuss cornering the market on security here in Magic City."

She shook her head. "Oh, it'll definitely be a party. But not one that you'll enjoy." Without instruction, the gathered magicals around her surged forward.

Jared yelled, "Go, go, go," and backpedaled, raising his rifle and looking for clean shots. Magical attacks deflected from the shields his people tossed up. The elf darted at him, and the riot shield she carried intercepted the bullets he sent at her. He growled, "Damn. I hate competent enemies."

She called, "Surely you didn't think we'd be unprepared for you to have anti-magic bullets? I mean, you must be at least marginally qualified to have lasted this long."

He muttered, "I'll show you qualified." Louder, he said, "Scenario Charlie is a go."

Ahead of him, the magicals fell back and created a wall to guard their retreat. They backed into the hallway they'd used to get there, moving carefully but quickly. The infomancer warned, "Masks on," and the ones who weren't already wearing breathing protection took a moment to set it in place.

The building's fire suppression system went off, clouds of gas billowing everywhere. Jared ordered, "Pop smoke," and he and his people tossed canisters in each intersection they passed through, maximizing the disruption of lines of sight. On their goggles, a blueprint map of the place showed their location. His team moved to their assigned positions, each human supported by at least one magical, ready for their opponents to advance.

When the first enemy appeared, a hulking Kilomea

gripping two riot shields in position to cover him high and low, Jared palmed a fragmentation grenade. He announced, "Free to engage," hurled the canister forward, and ducked around the corner. It detonated and pulled a shout of pain from the Kilomea, who hadn't tracked the bank shot off the wall that put the weapon behind him through the smoke. Jared grinned. "Let's get him."

Grentham had led his team up the first flight of stairs to the second floor. Scimitar was deep enough in the system now that she could warn him of technological traps, and with the anti-magic emitters running there was no risk of the other kind, so they made good speed. His subordinate in the lobby reported, "Contact," with the sound of rifles chattering behind him. A moment later, the man said, "Clear. I'm guessing they won't try that again."

Grentham shook his head. "Don't be too sure. Could've been recon. Find new positions and be ready."

His group encountered a pair of defenders, two elves who came around the corner at them in a dead run through the smoke his team had been tossing as they advanced. The enemies' shields intercepted the bullets fired in reflex, then they slammed into the dwarf at the head of the party, knocking him sprawling. A gurgle followed a scream, and he saw the flash of metal in one of their hands.

"Melee," he ordered, and the troops he'd detailed to engage in hand-to-hand combat pulled out weapons and surged ahead at their foes. A brief flurry ended with both elves down, along with another one of his people. "Potions, now." Two of his team peeled off to assist the fallen, two more went to make sure the elves were out of the fight, and he ran ahead with those remaining.

They were attacked twice more as he moved toward the rear of the building, then a final trio of enemies appeared in a hallway with big glass panes providing a full view of the garage below. Only one figure remained there, the elf, apparently coordinating her troops' efforts from the rear. He grinned. "No one appreciates someone who leads from the back. I think I need to go explain that to her."

Jared replied, "The elf lady?"

"Yeah."

"Kick her ass."

"Happy to." In truth, happy was exactly what he felt as he smashed his rifle against the window, shattering it, and jumped through.

Jared's first inclination was to assist his partner, but Scimitar's voice distracted him. "Armory is unlocked. Third floor, back corner."

He directed his team toward the stairs. "I'm going to need a portal to move that stuff. I don't care where, we can move it again afterward. Everyone not engaged in combat, head for the armory." A path appeared on his goggles, courtesy of the infomancer, and he trusted the same was true for all his people. When he arrived at the room containing the security company's equipment, it was like Christmas, and his face split into a grin. "They're definitely not using this place as a front. There's a ton of stuff here. You don't know what you're missing, partner."

Grentham, who had used magic to break his fall and spent the next several minutes trading blasts of fire, lightning, and shadow with his opponent, growled, "Little busy here. Let me know when you're all clear."

The elf looked annoyed, and her formerly pristine leather was now scarred and singed. He'd managed to slice off one of her braids, which had made her growl and him laugh. *Although, I suppose I'd be just as upset if someone chopped off a hunk of my beard.* He called, "Sure you don't want to call this done and partner up?"

She replied with a force blast that caught him in the shoulder and spun him around. He finished the turn by snatching an ax from his belt and pitching it sidearm at her. She'd abandoned her shield early in the fight since it was useless against magic, and waved a hand to deflect the weapon before it got to her. He charged, then dropped and slid as she produced throwing knives from nowhere and hurled them at his face. "Nice move," he said as he popped to his feet. "But not nice enough."

He called his ax back to his left hand and shot lightning at her with his right, landing a glancing blow as she dove to the side to avoid it. The interplay of electricity and muscles impacted her roll, leaving her sprawled on the ground. He threw the ax again, and it sliced a gash in her thigh as she twisted away. She clamped a hand over the wound and limped to her feet, and he rewarded her perseverance with a blast of fire that coated her completely.

When his magic dissipated, she was undamaged inside a force cocoon. He blasted her again, and again she protected herself. He observed, "I can do this all day, but if you take your hand off that wound to heal it properly, you'll probably bleed out before you manage it. So, it seems to me like eventually you're going to succumb."

She shook her head. "I'll outlast you, dwarf."

He summoned his ax, sticking it in his belt. "So you say. That assumes I don't have any other plans, which, of course, I do." A moment before, Jared had reported that they were done clearing up the armory and were evacuating the building. "Scimitar, let's wrap this up."

She replied immediately, "Vans are in position. Fifteen seconds."

Grentham grinned and dashed away from the elf, casting a portal ahead of him. He shouted, "See you later, assuming you survive." He dove through the rift an instant before the quartet of vans, each loaded with a truly excessive amount of explosive, slammed into the four sides of the building and detonated.

CHAPTER EIGHTEEN

Ruby selected a portal spot far enough away from Margrave's front door that Daphne could get the full impact of all the techno-magical items in his yard. He'd added a new one, a Halloween-style vampire that waved its arms and said, "Blah, blah, blah," as they walked by. The grin on its face, though, was unquestionably Margrave's, and she wondered if he was doing it in real-time or if he'd simply programmed the expression. *I need to figure out how he does this stuff. I guess having decades' worth of experience gives you some unique abilities.*

He opened the door for them when they reached the end of the sidewalk, and she introduced her companion. "Daphne, this is Phineas Margrave the Fourth, techno-mancer extraordinaire. Margrave, this is Daphne, one of my roommates and a brilliant witch. She's working on some potion improvements, and I thought maybe the two of you could confer while we work."

One side of the man's mouth lifted in a smile. "Techno-mancer? Is that what the kids are calling it these days?"

Ruby shook her head. "Not as far as I know, but I like the term, and it seems accurate, so why not?"

He nodded. "I humbly accept this title." Then he broke into his normal grin. "Okay, come inside."

He had wrangled drinks and snacks, and they sat and made small talk for ten minutes while they put it away. Ruby ventured, "I noticed a couple of new defensive measures in the yard. Cameras? Detectors?"

He finished chewing his oatmeal cookie and swallowed. "Yes, those. Nothing active outside, of course, just detection." The way he said it suggested that he'd beefed up his home's interior defenses, a decision she thoroughly supported. *One I need to do at our house, too.*

Daphne asked, "What are you working on?"

He adopted an imperious tone and replied, "You might as well ask a magician for the secrets of his tricks." Then he laughed and continued, "Some stuff for the government and the military, actually, so you'll have to keep it to yourself."

Daphne nodded. "No problem. I wouldn't want anyone leaking my work, either. I totally understand."

He cleared the dishes away and carried over a couple of boxes, removing his tools and components from it. Daphne did the same with the contents of her backpack, which included her burner, a small cauldron, and several potion bottles. Ruby hadn't brought anything to work on, planning instead to assist Margrave. She explained, "I do what I can to help him with this stuff, figuring I'll learn a bunch by doing so. So far, that's worked out really well."

Margrave snapped his fingers and stood, then grabbed another container. "You can start by taking a look at this.

It's a, uh, special forces weapon, for eliminating enemies non-lethally."

Ruby's ears perked up at that. *Well, I guess my team and I are special, and we're a force, so technically accurate.* She opened the hard-shelled black briefcase and took out the items nestled inside. A flexible strap held five tubes, one different from the others. She asked, "The closed one goes on the bottom?"

Margrave nodded, busy unpacking his other box. She strapped on the weapon. It fit perfectly around her upper forearm, which meant it would have to go on a little lower when she was in costume. Nestled in four separate cutouts were long, thin darts. Each was cut with grooves and had a point on the end that looked decidedly sharp and somewhat fragile. Even though she knew the answer, she asked, "What are they?"

He replied, "Knockout darts. They're aerodynamic by design, and the grooves help them spin as they leave the barrels to give them better accuracy. The payload is a drug that will cause instant paralysis, then render the target unconscious for a while, depending on their size and species and so forth."

Daphne frowned. "You're making a weapon to use against magicals?"

He shook his head. "I'm making a nonlethal tool for use against *anyone*. Better that than having to shoot your target and risk killing them, right?"

The witch considered the question for a second, then nodded. "Makes sense." She went back to setting up her cauldron and slipping her flasks into a small collapsible frame she'd assembled that supported them at an angle.

Ruby slipped one of the darts into place, happy to confirm that the spiky point didn't stick out. "Compressed air?"

Margrave replied, "Yep. Same stuff they use in paintball guns, but at significantly higher pressure and miniaturized. It's going to take some high-end precision equipment to replicate it on any serious scale, but that's not my problem."

Ruby laughed. "Create it, ship it, forget it. That's your motto, right?"

He nodded. "I've added a line, which is, 'on to the next.' Unless you have questions or concerns about that device, you can pack it up, and we'll do just that thing."

She shook her head and put the items away. "Looks great to me."

Daphne changed the subject. "So, I'm working on something that's only magic although there's a little chemical angle to it as well."

He nodded. "Tell me." She went on to explain what she was trying to do, increasing the "pop" of energy potions at an economy that would make it profitable, and they exchanged ideas for a couple of minutes. Ruby hadn't known Margrave was as versed in chemicals as he seemed to be, but it made sense. Like everything else when working in physical science, it was virtually impossible to avoid any of the various subfields completely. He offered her a few pointers and provided some supplies for her to run tests. She hummed happily, probably unaware she was doing so, as she worked with her components.

Ruby shook her head and slid the case with the dart

bracelet back to him. "Whoever gets that is going to be pleased with it, I think."

"I hope so." He handed over something in a closed fist, and she accepted it and peered at it under the table. It was a new version of the stun knuckles, with a little more protrusion at the points. "Nice. Fancy."

"More than that, it can be charged with lightning or plugged in."

"So, you can refuel it in the field?"

He nodded. "Exactly."

Ruby handed it back over to him. "That's handy. Very handy."

He grinned. "Okay, here's the real prize." He opened the big case he'd brought out at the beginning, revealing several items nestled in foam cutouts. One of them looked like a syringe gun straight out of a James Bond film.

She asked, "Are you making movie props now? Is Dr. Evil coming by for that later?"

"Har, har, har." He lifted the object and slid a small capsule into the barrel. "Give me your arm."

What the what? Still, she trusted him as much as anyone on Earth, so she extended her right arm. He set the injector against it and pulled the trigger, and a sharp pain was the result. It quickly faded, and she saw a small bulge under her skin. "What is it?"

"That one's a gel capsule. It'll dissolve in a day or so. I wanted to demonstrate the injector. The rest of these, though, are locator beacons."

Her eyes widened. They'd talked about such a device after the kidnapping at the casino, but she hadn't realized he'd started developing it. "Did you get it working? The casino owners in Magic City will probably pay a lot to have their kids trackable, given the current situation."

He nodded. "I'm a little uncomfortable with the whole thing since surveillance isn't really something I embrace. If it's opt-in, and the device is magically and technologically encrypted to a single receiver we can keep the Paranormal Defense Agency away from, it seems like a valid possibility. Ideally, you'd inject it somewhere no one would notice."

Daphne snarked, "Ruby has a boyfriend now, in case you weren't aware. I don't think there's *anywhere* it might not be noticed."

Margrave laughed, and Ruby ordered, "Shut it, or we'll test it out on your forehead."

He replied, "No, no, it has to go somewhere fleshy. Hitting bone with the injector would be bad for everyone involved."

Ruby argued, "All the more reason to try it there if you ask me."

Daphne stuck out her tongue, and Ruby shifted her attention back to Margrave as he spoke again. "I already have one injected in my thigh. So far, after a couple of days, no ill effects. Of course, I thoroughly tested it. Maybe you could take it, show it to your father?"

She nodded. *Take it and use it on my team and my parents, you mean.* "Will do. I'm sure he'll be enthused."

With a flourish, he produced one more object, a silver canister about the size of his hand. "This may be the coolest thing I've ever made. It's an EMP, very short range, probably just enough power to take out a single car, and it's both charged and activated by magical lightning."

Ruby shook her head, suppressing the desire to snatch

it from his hands and run away with it. "You've outdone yourself. Although, I imagine the military will want a more standard version."

"This one is more or less proof of concept. I'm not ready to hand this off to them just yet." He turned to Daphne. "What I could really use are healing and energy potions designed to absorb through the skin. Then, someone could wear them underneath their clothes and strike them to release the dose or something. The delivery mechanism wouldn't be hard once we had the right formula."

Her roommate virtually glowed at the suggestion. "I would *love* to work on that with you."

He nodded. "You're welcome anytime, with or without the sourpuss over there."

His reference acknowledged the frown that had snuck onto Ruby's face. She'd checked her watch and realized she had only a half-hour before she had to be at Spirits for the work gig that allowed Daphne to continue her research free of other commitments. She rose and said, "I have family stuff at the casino. I'll drop by and pick things up later. Is that okay?"

Margrave nodded. "Perfect." Daphne didn't reply, already lost in her research again. *It's worth every minute to see her finally focused on what she loves, even though I don't have an abundance of minutes to spare.*

CHAPTER NINETEEN

After her shift at Spirits, Ruby had decided to raid her parents' fridge for a late-night snack and crash at their place. She was comfortably sleeping the next morning when a knock on her door woke her up. She snarled, "What?" Then she realized where she was and said, "I mean, come in?"

Matthias stepped into the room and reported, "There's a messenger for you at the front entrance. They'll only speak directly to you, I'm sorry."

Ruby cocked her head to the side. "Any indication of what it's about?" He shook his head. She lowered her voice and asked, "Is it a police officer or government agent?"

He laughed. "Of course not. It's one of the runners the shopkeepers use to send messages back and forth."

"Kind of early, isn't it?"

His grin widened. "It's eleven in the morning."

She scowled. "Okay, I can feel your judgment over here. Go on, get out, tell him I'll be there in a minute." Idryll let out a meow as she stretched in her feline form as if to reinforce the order.

He replied, "Certainly," and stepped out.

Ruby threw off the covers, changed into shorts and a T-shirt that she hadn't slept in, and ran a brush through her hair. "I wonder what this is about?"

The cat on the bed observed, "Doesn't seem like an emergency, anyway. Although you probably inspired some questions by asking about police and agents."

She frowned at her reflection. "Yeah, yeah. I know. Brain's taking a little longer than usual to get online today."

"It's always difficult when you restart something you haven't used in so long."

"Oh, you're hilarious." She twisted and tossed the brush at the bed in a gentle arc, forcing Idryll to scramble out of the way. *Guess I'm lucky she didn't switch forms and throw it back at my face.* "Let's go see what the messenger has to say."

The mystery turned out to be a summons to visit Shentia, so after bidding the young courier goodbye, they headed for her shop. "Maybe she has something exciting to show us. I love new toys."

Idryll, now in her normal form and disguised by illusion, replied, "You should get some claws. Much better than punching, and I could teach you how to use them." Her tone wasn't even remotely playful.

Ruby nodded. "I'm open to that idea if we can find some that extend and retract like Wolverine's. Well, not actually into the skin, but gloves or something. I couldn't wear them full-time, though. The trouble twins would be insulted." Her artifact sword had become increasingly vocal about the fact that she didn't use the weapon as often as they'd prefer.

Idryll snorted. "Probably best to keep them happy since they're helpful with that thing in your arm."

She touched it involuntarily, then forced her hand aside. Fortunately, it looked enough like a real tattoo that she wasn't uncomfortable walking around with it out in the open. Nylotte had assured her that as long as she kept up her basic barriers, which so far she'd been able to do whenever she was awake, it would keep others from sensing the artifact unless they were particularly adept. Her tone when she'd said so had made Ruby think that not many people achieved that level of competency on the Dark Elf's scale.

They entered Shentia's shop and found her waiting, comfortably seated in a chair. The Drow nodded at their entrance and waved toward another nearby seat. Idryll beat her to it, and Ruby sat on the arm of the chair, squashing Idryll's arm against it before the tiger-woman pulled it out from under her with a growl. In here, she could let the illusion drop and allow Idryll to appear in her natural state. Ruby asked, "What can I do for you?"

Shentia smiled. "Funny you should phrase it like that because indeed, I have a task to request of you."

Ruby stilled her expression while her mind yelled, *I don't have time for this.* She'd promised to help whenever the Drow asked her to, and it was bound to come due, eventually. Worse, it would be impolite and potentially offensive to try to find out how much of her debt accepting the task would work off. Instead, she nodded. "Of course. Tell me what you need."

The Dark Elf steepled her fingers before her. She looked more severe than usual. "I was to have received possession of some property. However, someone stole it in transit. It's important to me, and I would like you to retrieve it."

Doesn't sound so hard, must be a catch somewhere. "What's it look like?"

"It's inside a carved wooden box, about the size of a large dictionary of your language."

Ruby shook her head. "Sorry, that doesn't tell me anything. You're aware of computers, right?"

Shentia sighed. "It's about as long as your dagger, bigger than that in the opposite rectangular direction, and about as high as four of them stacked on top of each other."

"Okay, sounds good. Are you tracking it?"

The other woman shook her head. "It was never in my possession to do so. However, I can get you to within a few blocks based upon the information the sender has provided."

Not very effective customer service on the sender's part. Figures. "Good enough. We'll change clothes and get started on it right away."

As they crouched on the rooftop across from the third warehouse they'd be checking for evidence of the stolen property, Idryll said, "Explain to me again why we're doing this in the middle of the afternoon."

Ruby's costume was hot. She was uncomfortable and irritated and sensed her companion both knew it and deliberately took advantage of it. She managed to keep the growl from her voice when she replied, "We don't want them to move it on us. Sounds like the seller isn't particularly good at keeping track of their stuff, and disappointing Shentia isn't an option. So, going after it right away makes us look better."

"It also makes this whole thing far more dangerous."

Ruby chuckled. "First, you don't think *anything* is particularly dangerous, so you're just being a jerk. Second, we'll go in quietly, take what we need to take, and get out of there. No muss, no fuss." The dart launcher was strapped onto her forearm, resting comfortably above the shield bracelet on that arm. They'd come fully ready to fight, but she truly hoped it wouldn't be required. *No muss, no fuss, please give me a break for once.*

Making sure her veil was solid, she blasted herself across the two-lane industrial street that ran between the buildings, then opened a portal for Idryll to join her. Probably the tiger-woman could've made the jump, but Ruby didn't want to take any unnecessary risks. They scuttled over to look down through the skylights, and Ruby muttered, "Bingo." Below lay a large room full of tables. On those surfaces were an assortment of items, some magical, some mundane, all probably stolen. Numerous magicals moved through the space, interacting with the objects. She spotted Kilomea, a couple of dwarves, and several Dark Elves in the slice of warehouse visible through the glass. "Wonder if someone down there is one of Shentia's competitors?"

Idryll shrugged. "Could be. So, do we go in fighting?"

Ruby scowled. "What part of stealth don't you understand? Besides, if it's special enough for Shentia to want it and someone else to steal it, the best place to check is probably the office."

"How do you know there's an office?"

She rolled her eyes and wondered what that looked like on the dragon mask's face. "These places *always* have an office, so whoever's in charge can get away from the workers. It'll be on one end, and if there's a second floor, on the second floor." Her prediction proved correct in both positioning and height. They opened the closest skylight and slipped through, Ruby carefully maintaining the illusion of normalcy and keeping them invisible while they descended to the steel frame a couple of feet below.

They crawled along the girders to the raised area containing the office and dropped to the staircase that led to the door. Ruby said, "We go in. I shoot whoever's in there with a dart. They go down. We take their stuff. We get out of here."

"I'm sure it'll work out just like that. Good to be an optimist." The sarcasm was thick. "Ready when you are."

She turned the handle and pushed the door open with her left hand, raising her right as she stepped through. A Dark Elf man in a dark suit sat behind a desk, sorting through a stack of papers. On the surface to his right was the box Shentia had described. *Dang, dictionaries are big.* She tapped the contact in her palm with the one on her ring finger to launch the dart, and it sped toward the magical. He waved a hand, and the projectile diverted to slam into the wall behind him. He took no additional actions other than to say, "I thought taking this powerful an object might spark your interest. I wanted to meet the last member of your gang."

Idryll growled, "You again. Not wandering down alleys to set ambushes for humans today?"

Ruby understood who it was, then. She said, "We're not a gang."

He nodded, leaned forward slightly, and rested his forearms on the desk. "Actually, you are. Several members, common cause, of interest to the authorities. Maybe you should get a dictionary."

Ruby closed her eyes and counted to three before responding. "You know, aged, arrogant Drow are starting to get on my nerves today. Maybe you should take that as a warning. I'm here. What do you want?"

He shrugged. "The humans in this town have overstepped and will continue to do so unless we rein them in. We need to make sure that anyone who takes action against a magical gets put in their proper place, hard. We won't go on offense, as such, but our defense must be brutally effective so that only a few lessons are needed to teach them all."

Idryll replied, "Their 'place' being in a coffin, right?"

He chuckled. "We could incinerate them so there are no remains to deal with, if you prefer."

Ruby shook her head. "We work within the law."

He scoffed, "Hardly. If you did so, you wouldn't have the police, the sheriff, and the lovely Paranormal Defense Agency tracking you."

She let out a long sigh. "This conversation is going nowhere. Do we need to take the box from you by force?"

He shook his head, then turned and opened the carved container so they could see the ornate dagger inside. "No, take it and go. I got what I wanted from it." She nodded, grabbed it, and backpedaled warily, with Idryll leading her. She paused before the exit to reactivate her veil, and at that moment, the Drow leaned forward and hit them both with a force blast, sending them tumbling backward to fall over the railing. His magically amplified voice shouted, "Get them."

CHAPTER TWENTY

Ruby twisted and controlled her descent with a burst of force magic that settled her onto her feet in perfect balance. Idryll had landed cleanly a foot away and was already charging the nearest foes. She pulled her eyes from the tiger-woman and focused instead on the pair of elves approaching from the right. *Holding this box is going to hamper my fighting ability.* She summoned her force shield, layering it above her skin, and drew the sword from over her shoulder.

The blade rang as it cleared its scabbard and the two oncoming enemies skidded to a halt, perhaps deciding that hand-to-hand wasn't as great an idea as they'd first thought. The first blasted her with lightning, and the second sent a wash of flame over her. She ran to her left, counting on her shield to handle the incoming attacks. They gnawed at her protection, sending pain as a reminder that even magical defenses weren't invulnerable. She sheathed the sword to the displeasure of the pair inside it, who muttered curses at her until she released the hilt.

Ruby cross-drew her dagger and turned back toward her foes, who had pounded in pursuit. She pointed the weapon and summoned a corona of lightning around the elves, then growled in frustration as their shields popped into place to protect them. *Dammit, I hate competent enemies.*

Idryll's instincts sent her running toward battle instead of away from it. It was simply a part of who she was, a key element of her psychological makeup, perhaps. All she knew, dashing forward with reckless abandon at the pair of Kilomea in front of her, was that her senses thrilled with the idea of the fight to come. She considered taking it up a level by using her claws, but Ruby hadn't given the go-ahead, and she could always turn to them at need if things went badly.

The first stepped forward with his fists raised like a boxer, clearly experienced and ready to mix it up. Instead of answering him in kind, she feinted a punch and kicked at his knee, going for the quick elimination. He dropped that knee to the floor, took her blow on his thigh, and grabbed her leg. She leapt off the other foot, aiming it in a kick at his head as she twisted in midair along her long axis in an effort to wrench the trapped foot from his grasp.

He released her and moved into a rising backpedal to avoid the blow, and she landed on her back to see the second Kilomea chopping down with a two-handed hatchet. It was more like something you'd use against a tree than a battle ax to use against a person, but the difference seemed largely irrelevant as the well-honed blade descended. She wrenched herself to the side and whipped an arm out to deflect it, managing to redirect it enough that it slammed into the concrete floor beside her head. The impact sent chips of stone flying, one of them carving a line across her cheek and narrowly missing her eye.

Her response was automatic, instinct taking the lead again. She extended the claws on her other hand and raked them down his arm, starting as far up as she could reach and ending at his wrist. They plowed a quartet of bloody furrows through his leather top and into his flesh. He jolted away with a shout of pain and surprise.

Time didn't permit her to revel in her success, however. The first Kilomea stomped down and smashed her knee against the floor, her last-instant twist the only thing that kept the joint from shattering. As it was, something was at least damaged, based on the fiery anguish that washed up through her. She threw herself into a backward somersault, rising smoothly on her good leg, resting the other on the ground enough to see if it would support her weight. It did, with a blaze of agony, but she wouldn't trust it. Instead, she extended the claws on her other hand, grinned around the blood trickling into her mouth from her torn cheek, and snarled, "Okay, playtime's over. Bring it."

Ruby's options were decidedly limited. She turned and ran again, this time toward Idryll, who appeared to be injured. A dwarf interposed himself along her path, sending lightning crackling out at her, and she slapped her bracelets together to summon another shield without stopping. She wanted to portal away and cursed herself for not having made the time to set up a safe receiving area. *First thing I'm going to do when I have any sort of gap in my schedule. Top priority.*

As it stood, she doubted her ability to get through an escape rift without the others following her through it or at the very least identifying where she went. Worse, all the places she would choose to go to were *not* places she wanted enemies to know about. *Sure, I could go out to the middle of the desert, to the collapsed motel or something. For all I know, that would be walking into a trap. No telling if they've been watching me, or for how long, or if they're part of the attack from before. Too damn many unknowns.*

She guessed it was an internal streak of conservatism that caused her to feel uncomfortable simply leaping into the unknown, even if it might turn out better than the current situation. *At least not until I have to.* She bowled the smaller figure over, ramming a knee into his chest when he tried to dodge. The blow stole her momentum, and she made a turning spin and dipped a hand toward the throwing dagger in her boot. The realization that she didn't want to have to leave the weapon behind when an opportunity to break away arrived stopped her from drawing it, and she growled at her indecision. *Quit being an idiot, Ruby. Do something.*

She lifted her arm, pointed the dart gun at the nearest Kilomea, who was raising a wicked-looking ax over his head and hit the pad to launch it. The dart flew true and stabbed him in the cheek. He paused, blinked in seeming confusion, then crumpled to the floor. She whispered a quiet thank you to Margrave and continued moving toward her partner.

Idryll had noticed Ruby headed in her direction and had opted for delay rather than continued provocation. When the one with the hatchet went down though, she launched herself at the Kilomea who had damaged her knee. He got his arms up to defend his face, but that wasn't her target. She transformed into her tiger form in mid-jump, her size increasing to something more appropriate for dealing with him, and slammed into the Kilomea with enough force to send them both flying.

She landed on top of him with a growl. He punched at her nose, and she grabbed the arm in her teeth and wrenched it, biting down. She stopped short of yanking and gnawing hard enough to sever the limb, but he definitely wouldn't be able to use it again without some serious medical attention. She roared into his face, causing him to blink uncertainly. He was unprepared when she slammed her forehead down onto his, channeling all the strength in her back and neck into the strike, knocking him unconscious.

The transformation had lessened the pain in her knee, but she was still limping as she climbed off his still body and moved toward her partner. Ruby had drawn her pistol and held it extended as she backed slowly toward the door. She said, "I need you to have hands."

Idryll smoothly transitioned back into her humanoid form and took the box. Ruby cast a force barrier in front of her, and when their enemies surged forward, fired the gun through a small hole in the shield. The anti-magic bullet passed through unhindered to slam into the leg of the nearest. She called, "That was a warning. Anyone who gets near us before we get out of here, dies. I guarantee I have enough bullets for all of you, not to mention what my partner's carrying."

From the staircase near the office, the Dark Elf's laughter rang out. "Let them go." He shifted his gaze down to them. "I wanted to see what you both were made of. Nice claws, cat lady."

Idryll gave him a bloody smile. "Don't forget the teeth."

He nodded. "Indeed, very impressive. You've both proven you're competent and thus dangerous. Consider what I said. Those qualities can protect the magicals in Ely if you choose to employ them properly. You should definitely do so."

Idryll opened the exterior door and backed through it, slamming it closed after Ruby joined her outside. Her partner created a portal to a street Idryll recognized near the wreckage of the Mist casino, and they both jumped through. On the opposite side, a drone swooped down on them, and Idryll tensed her muscles to jump away if it started to shoot. Instead, it hovered there.

Ruby snarled, "Invasion of privacy. It's recording us." She flipped it off. "See, this is why portals are a problem." Idryll followed as her partner jogged down the road, confident that they'd soon be veiled and portaling home. *After all that fighting, I need a snack.*

CHAPTER TWENTY-ONE

It wasn't often anymore that Ruby visited her father's office at Spirits, but every time she did, she was struck by how impressive the surroundings were. *If I didn't know him so well, I might even think* he *was impressive.* She snorted inwardly. *He's amazing, a natural-born leader, and everybody knows it. How's* that *for something to live up to?*

Daphne also looked impressed. The witch's introduction to her father had been down in one of the lower offices used for less important meetings. Her roommate seemed nervous, and Ruby poked her. "Chill out. It'll be great, whatever you have to say."

Daphne nodded, but her level of agitation didn't change. She'd refused to share any information ahead of time, claiming the professional thing to do would be to let her employer know first. Ruby thought that was a little over-the-top, given that the woman was an insatiable gossip about most other things, but she wasn't about to argue. *It's her show. However she wants to do it is fine.*

Her father arrived and shook hands with Daphne on his

way around the desk. He plopped into his chair and smiled at the two of them. "So, what do you have for me today?"

Her roommate straightened and squared her shoulders, then reached into the bag at her feet. She pulled out a flask, similar in size to the thing heart patients carried on their keychains filled with nitroglycerin pills. She handed it over, and he examined the object from several angles. "This is?"

She replied, "An energy potion with about twenty-five percent of the effectiveness of a full one, at one-sixth the size."

He nodded with an expression of approval. "Does it scale up?"

"Only to about a hundred and ten percent of the original, for some reason. I managed some improvement there, but my efforts mostly focused on reducing the volume most effectively."

He set it on the desk, rolling it slightly with a fingertip. "So, what market do you see for this?"

She smiled and launched into an obviously rehearsed speech. "I think it's broken down by demographic. For the eighteen to say thirty-five crowd, it can be something they carry around to extend whatever good time they're having. It has no negative interactions with any other substance anyone's reported, so if they've had a drink or two and need a little boost to keep going, no problem."

She paused and waited for him to nod, then continued. "For the slightly older crowd, say, thirty-five to sixty, it can be a refresh during the workday, or later when it's time to be with family. Finally, those sixty-plus can use it to enhance the day whenever they want. Obviously, it'll be situational in all these cases, but who couldn't use a little hit of energy now and again?"

Rayar smiled. "That sounds like a good marketing slogan to me. Is it addictive?"

Daphne shook her head, her smile gone. "Physically, no. Psychologically, no more so than a full potion, I would imagine. Although since this will be less expensive, there could be some concern there."

He nodded thoughtfully. "That's why we have lawyers. I could see a lot of applications for this in the military and law enforcement, too. I think you have a winner here. So, what do you want to do with it next?"

"I thought we could start marketing it to a test group at a discount, get their responses, that sort of thing. I don't really know much about marketing." She was almost apologetic.

Ruby's father laughed. "Fortunately, since casinos are *all* about marketing, we have a ton of people who are experts in that discipline. We can use Spirits for distribution, maybe make a game or contest out of it."

Ruby replied, "Or a comp for high rollers. Keep them at the tables a little longer."

He nodded, then frowned as he reconsidered. "No, that seems like a great idea at first, but it opens us to accusations of artificially manipulating their spending. The legal team would never sign off on it."

She laughed. "That's what the whole comps program in every casino is about, isn't it? But I get your point. This isn't quite the same. Offer it to the employees? Give them a little bonus if they volunteer?"

"It's worth thinking about." He shifted his gaze to

Daphne. "In any case, we'll find a test group so we can get feedback for both marketing and other concerns. Have you had this examined by a medical professional?"

The witch shook her head. "No, but I totally agree that should be something we do."

He rolled the cylinder to Ruby, who caught it as it plummeted off the table. "During your next shift, you can escape the casino and consult with our medical contractors."

She nodded, and Daphne said, "Wait. You work here?"

Ruby chuckled. "A bit."

"Where do you find the time?"

She shrugged but with a smile. "Here and there, wherever I can fit it in. Fortunately, the boss is pretty flexible on my schedule." She gestured at her father, then put her hand in front of her mouth and whispered loudly, "He doesn't know I only come here to sleep."

Rayar asked, "You weren't aware my daughter was working here one day a week?" Daphne shook her head. "Well, well, well. Interesting. I've been trying to get her to commit for ages, but it was only when I made it a condition of *your* gig that she agreed. So, even if you hadn't come up with something so wonderful, I'd still be in your debt."

Ruby grinned. "Now, Daphne, *you're* in *mine*." She said the last in a dark, evil tone, then broke into laughter at the concern on her roommate's face. "No, seriously, it's nothing to worry about. I negotiated a cut of the profits, so it's all good."

The other woman asked, "You're sure?"

Ruby shrugged. "As long as the conditions of the

arrangement don't change, I'm fine with it, or I wouldn't have signed on the dotted line."

Daphne chuckled. "Figuratively, of course."

Rayar shook his head. "Oh no. There's a contract. Ruby's too smart to trust anyone's word in a business deal."

Her housemate lifted an eyebrow. "Really? You're more of a shark than I thought."

More like a dragon, but sure. She shrugged. "I learned from the best. Now, tell me what you're going to do next to make us all some money."

Daphne replied, "Well, since I've figured out how to do it for energy potions, I thought it shouldn't be too tough to do the same thing for healing. The question is, volume first, or effectiveness?"

Morrigan finished her shift overseeing the high rollers area and rode the elevator up to her office to change. It had been a long day, most of it spent on her feet, and she looked forward to relaxing over a meal at the new restaurant at the gnome casino Invention with her best work friend, Stacia. She slipped out of the professional black dress she'd been wearing and into a pair of tight leather pants, high boots, and a flowing red silk top. She checked herself in the mirror and said, "*You* look like an interesting person. Doubtless, everyone will want to get *your* number." She snorted at her reflection and headed for the door.

She met up with Stacia on the casino floor, and they walked together out the front doors. Dusk was falling, and the casinos were like miniature suns. Light radiated out in all colors and directions, from the almost garish displays meant to lure people into the gaming area to the pale illumination of the hotel rooms in the high towers.

Stacia had changed as well, out of her pit boss uniform and into a little black dress that was definitely on the social side of the professional-social continuum. Morrigan said, "Damn, you're hot."

The other woman laughed and slapped her arm. "You're only complimenting me because you're trying to get out of paying for dinner."

Morrigan laughed. "Well, you're half-right. I always speak the truth, but I'm *also* trying to get out of paying for dinner."

Stacia shook her head. "Nope. You lost the bet, fair and square. I told you he'd be back." One of their high rollers had endured an impressive stretch of lucklessness the day before, and Morrigan had predicted he'd end his vacation early. To the casino's lasting benefit, she'd been wrong, but she owed Stacia a debt of honor in the form of an expensive dinner.

They moved to the far side of the Strip, close to the casinos along that edge, but not *too* near. Street crime wasn't frequent in Magic City, but when it happened, it was generally on the side streets that led to the town beyond the casinos. Her roving gaze caught sight of several drones overflying the area, the size and shape of Paranormal Defense Agency units. She scowled, then quickly banished the look and smiled at her friend. "What are you going to get?"

Stacia replied immediately. "Steak, the best cut they have since you're paying."

"Wench."

The other woman laughed at the insult and replied, "Jerkface."

A pair of guys in jeans and polo shirts who stopped at the sight of them interrupted their banter. The first, dark-haired one spoke to her. "Hey, Red. We're looking for an adventure. Want to join us?"

Morrigan shook her head. "Got plans already, thanks."

His companion, a blond with short spiky hair sticking out in all directions, aimed his comments at Stacia. "Aww, come on. Whatever you're doing, we can do it together."

Her friend laughed. "Probably a little rich for your blood, boys."

The first one smirked with an edge of ill humor. "Trust me, we're *men*, and we can handle any entertainment you might care to propose."

The blond stepped directly in front of Stacia, and she stopped short to avoid colliding with him. He urged, "Come on, let's talk about this."

Morrigan replied, "No means no, boys," stressing the last word.

Stacia grabbed her arm and pulled her toward the edge of the street. She said, "We can go in the employee entrance. I'll call someone to let us in." The men continued to stand there staring at them, and Morrigan considered whether she should beat them down as a matter of principle. Still, the Dark Elf's comments from the alleyway rang in her memory, and she couldn't. *They're scumbags, but words don't deserve violence in response.* Instead, she allowed Stacia to drag her onto the side street. The men followed, but at enough of a distance that they were no longer a factor beyond keeping them from veering back to the Strip.

Morrigan realized what that behavior indicated a moment too late. A trio of Kilomea appeared out of nowhere, and fists pummeled her into unconsciousness before she had time to summon a shield.

CHAPTER TWENTY-TWO

Ruby opened a portal directly into Demetrius's bedroom and pulled Margrave through when the older man didn't move fast enough to satisfy her. She snapped, "Did you find her?"

Demetrius shook his head and continued staring at his screens. His urgency was evident as his hands flew over the keyboards. Even if it had been the most intense concern he'd felt in his life, she was positive it wouldn't begin to match hers. The idea that someone had taken her sister caused her vision to go white and her temples to pound every time she thought about it. She was as angry as she'd ever been, the emotion tinged with fear, worry, and guilt.

Margrave asked, "Do you see the other locators?"

The infomancer pointed at the leftmost of his three screens, where tiny dots pulsed on a map. Ruby had injected the devices into herself, Morrigan, her brother, and her parents. Idryll had demurred, unwilling to have anything implanted into her. Ruby hadn't argued, figuring the shapeshifter knew her physiology best.

Margrave scratched his chin. "Obviously, the locators and tracker are working. The only logical conclusions, then, are that they got the locator out and destroyed it since we don't see it anywhere, or they have her in a place that's shielded from signals and magic. In that case, the emanations might be limited enough that we can't detect it from this distance."

Demetrius nodded. "I've been systematically uploading the software to cell towers and network hubs, but it's slow going since I have to do each one personally. You'd think they'd use a common algorithm, but no, the security appears to have been designed by a computer and is seriously randomized. There's a paper in that for some academic, probably."

Ruby snapped, "Focus, people. So, she's not close enough to here to locate her with the tracker. How do we find her?"

Margrave gave a sharp nod. "I'll make a portable version of the tracker. I already have the pieces at my place. It won't be pretty, and the battery will be darn heavy, but I can get it done in a couple of hours."

"Do it." He opened a portal to his house and departed. She turned back to stare at the screens. Nothing had changed. Her parents were together, no doubt watching the phone as she, Morrigan, and their mother had when Dralen and her father were missing. Her brother was at Spirits, probably in his office based on the location. The top-down map didn't indicate height or depth.

She shook her head. "Waiting for Margrave isn't enough. Hack all the databases. PD, Sheriff, PDA. I'll send Alejo an apology message while you work. Find whatever you can. I'm thinking street cameras, drones, maybe even incident reports, or beat cop body cams. Whatever's out there."

Demetrius replied, "Not my first rodeo, partner. If there's something there to be found, I'll find it. In the meantime, you need to go down to the kitchen and make us both sandwiches."

The request was so atypical of their relationship that a laugh escaped her. "What?"

"It's not a gender thing. You have to eat before whatever you're going to do when we find a lead, and I'm starving because I went straight from other work into this. If I don't get fed, I won't function as well. Same for you. You know the old military maxim. Eat when you can because there's no knowing what's coming next, or something like that."

She headed for the door, forced to acknowledge that he was correct on all counts. "Just don't think this is going to be a habit, mister."

He threw her a quick grin before she left. "If you keep owing me, it might be."

Fortunately, she didn't run into any of her other roommates as she assembled bread, ham, cheese, and spicy brown mustard into sandwiches, two for each of them. She cut a pair diagonally and the others vertically, not knowing which he preferred. Things like that didn't matter to her. Unless it was an amazing meal that one reveled in, food was merely fuel. She took them up, along with a couple of sodas, and quietly ate while he worked. Finally, when she was half-done with her second sandwich, he shouted, "Yes. Big screen."

Above the trio of monitors he used for his infomancy

was a large flatscreen. It was usually off, although she'd seen cartoons playing on it once or twice while he worked. They'd also watched a movie one night, managing to get all of five minutes into it before falling asleep together. Now, it showed a grainy image from a street camera overlooking the Strip. It lurched into motion as she shifted her attention to it, and her sister entered the frame, walking with another woman Ruby recognized from Spirits. No sound accompanied the video, and the low resolution suggested he had digitally zoomed it in from a distant spot. The pair walked down the Strip talking, and Ruby asked, "Where from?"

"Traffic camera on the other side."

As the image moved with the women, doubtless another digital trick, two men appeared. The angle showed only the backs of their heads, but Demetrius's software quickly calculated height and weight for each. She said, "Print those for me, and get the files to Alejo."

"On it." The image started to move again, and there seemed to be some back and forth between them. Ruby read the men's actions as aggressive and figured her sister would do the same. *So right now she's wondering whether she should blast them into unconsciousness with some lightning. Of course, that would cause a scene and bring the police, and Morrigan Achera isn't known to be a combative person. So, of course, she couldn't do that. They were counting on their target not wanting to cause a scene.* Out loud, she asked, "I don't see anything that confirms they deliberately targeted my sister, do you?"

He widened out the shot to reveal dozens of other people in proximity to the pair. "I think the chances are low that it was random. I mean, your sister's body language wasn't particularly open, and they had other choices when Morrigan didn't immediately accept them if they only wanted to get anyone."

She scanned the image and scowled. "They're the only pair of women together, but you're right. They could have targeted a single woman with much better results, or maybe two women who were part of a larger group. You're right. We'll assume this was a deliberate attack on her until something tells us differently."

The alarm had gone out as soon as they'd learned of the kidnapping, which fortunately had come fairly quickly when the pair missed their dinner reservation and the restaurant called Spirits to confirm. When Morrigan didn't answer the call from the office, it triggered a standard protocol that involved verifying the location of all the family members. When they discovered Morrigan still wasn't responding, the word went out to the other casino owners and their families to activate their contingency plans.

Demetrius said, "Okay, we're going to jump forward at least a few seconds. This angle is from a PDA drone. I grabbed all I could before I had to get out of the system or risk detection."

"I know you're giving it your all, Tree. I appreciate it. Someday I'll show you how much. For now, hit play." The scene started to move, and her sister walked into the mouth of the alley beside Invention. She muttered, "Why are you doing that, Morrigan?" He tapped to widen the view a little, and she spotted the employee entrance. "Okay, that had to have been their destination." The next section was in a jerking motion as if missing frames turned it into a series of pictures rather than a smooth video.

She watched as three people rushed into the frame. Despite the concealment offered by their masks, the figures were clearly Kilomea, their skin tone and body type making it impossible for them to be anything else. Anger surged inside as both women were beaten and dragged away. She took a moment to master the rage burning through her. "Can you get any closer? Try to find us something to identify those bastards?"

Demetrius filled the next three minutes by manipulating the image, zooming it in, zooming out, and moving along body parts. Finally, they caught a break. The motion froze, showing a mark on one of the Kilomea's arms where their shirt had ridden up above the wrist due to the struggle. The infomancer said, "Analyzing, hang on," before she could push him. A line drew itself over the mark and grew in resolution as the program ran. Eventually, the differently colored section revealed itself as a tattoo of a hunter's arrow, the point wickedly barbed, and the feathers a blur of poorly rendered computer squiggles.

"You're the best, Tree. What can you do with it?"

"Probably the most likely hit will be from the Strip. So, we'll use the surveillance cameras. Will you make some calls and get us access to the other casinos' systems so I don't have to break through their security?"

It took half an hour of arranging permissions and searching, but finally, they found a matching tattoo in a video shot several days before. The Kilomea in question was walking toward the front entrance of The Hunt with his uniform coat slung over his shoulder, the tattoo visible on his bare arm. Demetrius's technical wizardry overlaid the two tattoos, showing a match. He said, "Either this guy and the other one got the same ink from the same artist, or he's our target."

She replied, "It's a place to start. You keep working the systems. See what else you can find. I think it's time for me to go on the hunt for a hunter at The Hunt." *Even miserable, angry, and frustrated, I'm still completely hilarious. Really, Demetrius doesn't realize how lucky he is to be with me.*

CHAPTER TWENTY-THREE

Ruby did her best to maintain her calm. "No, you can't come with me. It's going to be hard enough managing my illusion in such a dramatically different form. I wouldn't be able to do it for both of us."

Idryll put her hands on her hips and shook her head. "You underestimate yourself."

She let out a dark laugh. "The only time you compliment me is when you know you're in the wrong. Give it up."

Her partner replied, "Logic suggests you'll need backup. Maybe I could use a physical disguise and go in that way. Or simply show up like this." She gestured at herself.

"Well, you'd certainly attract attention, given all that beautiful fur." A surge of darkness washed through her, and she sent a mental message to the passenger located in her left arm. *Knock it off, bastard. Now is not the time.* If she were smart, she'd spend the next hour meditating inside her protective ring as Nylotte had taught her. *No one ever accused me of being smart.* She had no time for anything other than exactly what was required to find and free her sister.

She said, "Don't worry, I have tasks for you. Margrave will be here as soon as he finishes the locator. If we haven't made any progress by then, you can go out scouting. If that's not viable, you can work with him to create a secure space here, warded against everything you can manage in a short time."

"Why?" Despite her irritation, the shapeshifter sounded interested.

"Landing pad. I figure if I open a portal in the field, and it's only to an empty room, anyone seeing through to it won't learn anything. If they're stupid enough to follow me in, the wards should shift any fight in my favor."

A note of grudging respect entered her companion's voice. "That's actually a really good idea."

"Don't worry. It wasn't mine. Margrave suggested it."

Idryll laughed. "That explains it."

Ruby was more than a little concerned about her ability to pull off what she had planned. Her self-control at the moment was tenuous and imitating a being far different than herself in size and form was precision illusion magic requiring serious levels of concentration. She had to eliminate every risk she could, which is why she was heading in wearing regular clothes rather than her costume. *That way, if my illusion does falter, it'll be easier to blend in.*

She put on jeans, a black tank top, and a flowing black button-down shirt over it that secured at her belly button. Her cuffs went over her bracelets, and she tucked her shield pendant into her shirt. She had no other magical objects she could easily hide on her person, and the Kilomea casino, like all the others, would have dramatically increased their vigilance after the events at the Mist. "I need some more stuff that's easy to disguise. Exploding pens, rings that shoot laser beams, that sort of thing."

A frown had crept onto Idryll's face as Ruby dressed. Her partner asked, "Won't your bracelets set off the new detectors?"

"Dammit." In her frenzy of preparation, she hadn't accounted for the new, more effective sensors that lined the entrances of all the casinos. She slipped off the cuffs and tossed them to Idryll. The other woman had another question at hand. "Will your illusion trigger it?" She'd be heading in as a random Mist Elf, with features garnered from a dozen different individuals to construct the identity.

She had several of those prepared in case she needed to be someone other than Ruby Achera the human or Ruby Achera the Mist Elf. "That illusion doesn't use too much magic, so hopefully it shouldn't cause a problem. If it does, I can explain it away as my heirloom pendant." She patted her chest. "Passed down to me from my grandmother, and her grandmother before her, and so on. I'm sure they'll respect such a historic item."

Idryll gave her a frown. "You should still take me with you. You know that, right?"

Ruby nodded. "I do know that. I can't do it this time." She grabbed the other woman's arm and squeezed it. "Think good thoughts for me. Hopefully, when we see each other again, I'll know where Morrigan is. You can be sure I won't leave you out of getting her back."

Idryll grinned. "Claws and teeth?"

Ruby nodded. "No quarter for whoever took her. Anyone who's left standing at the end of it should spend the rest of their days counting their blessings."

She portaled to an alley near The Hunt. Part of her hoped the kidnappers would make a move on her. *Of course, since I'm a nobody and they're probably after specific people, not too likely.* She walked forward, inserting herself into the trailing edge of a bunch of human women headed for the entrance. One of them wore a very sexy dress that resembled a wedding gown, so she chalked it up as a bachelorette party. That was one area where Magic City competed quite well with Vegas because the real or perceived touch of danger from being around magicals made that particular rite of passage all the more memorable.

She passed through the detectors with only a nod from the guard as if to say, "We know you're using magic, but we're not going to make a fuss about it right now. Don't cause trouble." The pit bosses at the casinos were exceedingly well-trained to detect signs of power in use, and anti-magic emitters at the tables meant she would need to chart her course through the casino carefully.

The interior resembled a thick forest with a canopy of branches and leaves high overhead. Trails meandered through the space, along with numerous signs offering directions to essentially everything. Unlike a normal casino, patrons couldn't see the entertainments that lay beyond their location. *I need to chat with whoever designed this someday. It's like the opposite of a good casino layout, but obviously it works. I wonder how they managed it.*

She wandered through the gaming floor, taking note of the different uniforms, matching them up against her memory of the garment the Kilomea she sought had carried over his shoulder. It didn't take long to discover that it was the top the casino's dealers wore. She inwardly groaned as she moved to an unoccupied corner and tapped her comm to activate it under the guise of scratching her ear. "Looks like it's part of a dealer's uniform. Which means I only have to check the whole damn place."

Demetrius replied, "Yeah, decidedly suboptimal, there. Do better."

She closed her eyes so no one would see them rolling. "Any chance of hacking in?"

"High risk of detection. Even though we got inside when we did our first search, I wasn't able to leave any back doors. You could call and ask?"

"No. I don't trust anything or anyone at this point. That'll be the backup plan."

She headed for the nearest restroom and locked herself in a stall. "Okay, Ruby, you can do this." She closed her eyes and imagined the Kilomea she'd assembled from magazine pictures and video recordings. The illusion grew around her body, making her look bulkier. The sort of clothes she'd seen nonworking members of that species wearing inside the casino faded into view, including heavy leather pants, boots, and tunic with long sleeves, all in various shades of brown. A deep green vest sat over top of it, leather again, left open. A weapons belt with empty sheaths for daggers finished the look.

She hadn't realized before entering that the casino required Kilomea to check weapons, but it made sense. Doubtless, it involved some careful negotiations since Kilomea heirlooms tended to be of the violent kind, passed down from one generation to the next. She unlocked the door and strode out, pausing only long enough to shoot a glance at her reflection to make sure nothing seemed out of place.

Walking through the casino in her new form was a unique experience. People moved out of her path in a way they never did for Ruby Achera in any of her guises. It was almost automatic, how they flowed to clear space for her. *I could get used to this.* She kept a careful distance from the anti-magic emitters, more than once having to turn and take a different route when two tables were sufficiently close together that she couldn't pass between them. After forty-five minutes of charting her course along the various paths in the forest, she was moving from deeply annoyed to downright angry. *When I find this bastard, I'm going to break every one of his teeth as a greeting.*

She imagined Keshalla's voice, asking, "Then how will he talk?"

Fine, hands then. That'll be even worse since he can't deal with broken fingers. She abruptly stopped as she spotted him and made a quick sidestep to avoid someone reacting to her motion. She growled, "Sorry," taking a position nearby and watching him without appearing to do so, waiting for the right moment.

Eventually, he set down the cards, made the sleeve

move and open hands display that showed he wasn't cheating, and left the table, presumably to take a break. She got ahead of him and brushed against him only hard enough to put the locator she'd palmed on his jacket. She didn't apologize to his irritated glare, merely nodded an acknowledgment of it. *Be seeing you, buddy.*

CHAPTER TWENTY-FOUR

Ruby had visited the ladies' room to reverse her disguise and exited out to wander the Strip. She looked like another person staring at their phone, but hers displayed her target's location, which had been moving around the casino in the hours since she'd tagged him. Normal shift switchover time was coming up soon, and she said a small prayer to the universe in the hope that he wasn't working a double. When he headed toward the employee exit, she heaved a sigh of relief and positioned herself to spot him when he emerged.

She considered going after him immediately, snagging him, and portaling away with him. However, the receiving room wasn't yet ready and wouldn't be for another hour or so. *Besides, maybe following him will lead to more information. I'm sure I won't get lucky enough that he'll take me to my sister, but one clue leads to the next, and all that.* Having verified he was truly out of the building, she muttered, "You got him?"

Demetrius replied, "Two drones. Both running conceal-ment, so the PDA shouldn't notice them."

"Excellent. Keep me apprised." She found a secluded spot and opened a portal to the middle of the desert, noting that the motel had burned down to its frame and what remained looked remarkably unstable. From there, she portaled to her office at Spirits, then to the bunker. She growled as she passed her friends, "Get that room done fast, people. I have a feeling we'll need it."

Margrave and Idryll tossed answers after her, but she had already left them behind, headed for the chamber holding her equipment.

After changing into her uniform and portaling back, she reacquired her target and followed him to a narrow apartment building. It was three stories high and only large enough to have one unit on each level. He entered and appeared to head for the stairs, and she released the tiny drone that was part of her gear. She piloted it around the structure, peering through every window. She reported, "Okay, three on the bottom, two in the middle, and the target plus one on the top."

Demetrius replied, "That's what I saw, too. Did you notice they all had pieces of casino uniforms lying around?"

"Yeah. Makes sense. Lower-level people often come here from out of town to take jobs and wind up rooming with others who work at the casino. That's a lot of Kilomea inside one building, though."

"Are you going to take them all out?" The words tumbled uncomfortably off his tongue.

"No. I only have two knockout darts left, and the ones I care about are on the top floor. I think if I put a shield around the apartment, it should block sound enough that the people at street level won't hear. Can't count on those in the middle unit not hearing, so they'll have to go first."

He replied, "Why bother knocking them out if you're probably able to lock in the sound?"

"Backup plans, my friend. Always have backup plans. And an exit. And a snack." She quit babbling and piloted the drone to a position where it offered a view of the inside of the second-floor apartment door. She left it hovering there and entered the building under a veil, climbing the stairs to that entrance. Using the reverse angle image, she called upon her force magic to slide the bolt quietly and turn the other two locks, muttering, "This is weird." The feed from the drone revealed one of the two had moved into the living room. The other, presumably, was still in the bedroom they'd been in originally. She inhaled a deep centering breath, focused her will past the anger and rage that wouldn't leave, and opened the door quietly.

The Kilomea on the couch turned from watching the television at her entrance, and she nailed him in the neck with a dart before he could do anything else. He slumped, and she retrieved the projectile and stuck it in her belt. She crept through the apartment, extending a sound shield so the ones above wouldn't hear if things went wrong.

She discovered the other in the bedroom, asleep. *Sorry, buddy.* His eyes flew open as the dart punched into his flesh, then they fluttered closed again as the drug took effect. She retrieved the evidence of her presence and moved to the window, sliding it up.

A fire escape led up to the third floor. She repositioned the drone, making sure she'd have a clean entrance on the next level, and confirmed that the bedroom proximate to the metal staircase was empty. She climbed most of the way but stopped before anyone could see her from the apartment. It took her five minutes of careful effort to layer the top floor of the building in shields without possibly alerting those inside, but when she finished, she was confident no sound would escape, and no one would break in to interrupt her.

She ascended the rest of the way and slid open the window, climbed through, and dropped into a crouch. Her veil was strong, and she had no doubt she'd be able to make her first attack by surprise. She didn't dare kill either of them, and she hoped for a quick punch with the stun knuckles to take out the roommate. *What will be, will be.* She said, "Going in. Keep an ear on the police band."

Demetrius gave her a click in reply. Their experience working as a team had taught him to minimize distractions when a fight was at hand. Ruby walked out to the living room, invisible to the apartment's occupants. She found them both there, throwing darts and drinking. They discussed innocuous things: work, women, plans for vacations. She wondered if the second Kilomea might have been one of the three and re-resolved not to kill him.

There didn't seem to be a way to separate the two, so finesse was pretty much out. She dashed forward, still hidden, and threw a punch at the roommate's face with her shock-enabled fist. Something gave her away. *The movement of air, maybe.* Instincts were a thing, and by all accounts, the Kilomea had excellent ones where hunting and fighting were concerned. He swept an arm out to deflect the blow and hurled the pair of darts in his left hand in her direction with a loud shout of alarm. She dropped the veil and summoned a force shield to block them, then lashed out in a kick. It caught him in the midsection and knocked him stumbling backward.

The other had reacted equally quickly, throwing his darts and dashing toward the small kitchen that lay a dozen feet away. She growled, "No knives for you," and hit him with a blast of force that sent him into the nearby wall with a satisfying *crunch*. *The more you hurt, the happier I'm going to be.*

The first was on his way in again, holding a knife. She dropped back into a boxer's stance, whipping out her left hand to knock his slash away and leaving it there to hold the arm in place when he tried a backhand stab. She slammed her fist into his ribs and the shock knuckles detonated with a loud *snap*. He stood, dazed, but didn't go down. *Dammit, fall, you jerk.* She snapped out a kick to send him tumbling toward the one that had snatched her sister, but that opponent deftly dodged the incoming Kilomea projectile and closed with her.

He charged for a bear hug, counting on his size to protect him. *Stupid move.* She blocked his arms out to open his torso and rammed a knee up at his groin. He shifted his thigh inward to catch the blow and snapped a fist at her face. She dove to the side to avoid it, judging that simply moving her head wouldn't be enough. When she came up, the Kilomea were both alert and seemed eager to fight. The one who'd snatched her sister said, "Look, Magic City's very own superhero. It'll be fun finding out who you are."

The other nodded. "And making sure you don't mess with anyone's plans again."

Ruby laughed. "I'm far from super, and I'm no hero.

However, I'm more than a match for the likes of you two idiots." She grabbed the lightning grenade from her belt and threw it at their feet. The energy surged around them, stiffening them both. She dashed in to the roommate and delivered a right cross to his temple. The stun blast was less powerful, given the drain from the previous punches, but landed in a much better spot. He went down hard.

The other one swung at her, and she ducked, stepping back. She spread her arms wide and said, "What's the matter? Can't manage to hit a girl half your size?"

He growled but didn't overreact to the taunt. Instead, he shuffled forward and delivered a flurry of punches so fast that she had no chance of picking each of them off individually. She summoned force shields on both forearms and positioned them in front of her, absorbing the blows and laughing at him until he stopped throwing them.

Ruby said, "So, I know you were there when the casino owner girl got kidnapped. You're going to tell me where she is. Easiest way to get that done is for you to confess."

He laughed darkly. "What, and you let me go?"

She shook her head. "That's not in the cards. You'll have to pay for your crime, no question. The only variable is whether you'll be mostly unbroken when the door of your cell clangs shut."

He growled, "I don't care how much magic you have. I'll beat you down just like I did that little tramp."

Red fury obscured her vision, and she expelled power like a tidal wave of vengeance. When she was able to see past the haze again, the Kilomea was writhing in agony on the floor. Shadow tentacles wrapped around his body, two of them pushing against vulnerable pressure points in his arms and another pair resting above his horrified eyes, ready to plunge in.

Inwardly, Ruby snarled, *No*. She mastered control of the tendrils but didn't retract them. Instead, she let them keep causing him pain. She smiled as she composed herself. "So, perhaps you've reconsidered your position?"

CHAPTER TWENTY-FIVE

Ruby sat cross-legged in her warded circle, getting her thoughts in order for the events to come. The Kilomea had given up the information quickly, but all he'd had to offer was a general location—Reno or somewhere nearby. Margrave's remote tracker was already there, in the hands of one of Diana's agents. *Man, I owe them a lot.* She pushed that thought away, storing it with all the other concerns that didn't relate to her sister. She needed purity of mind, especially after triggering the artifact against the Kilomea.

The item always left her feeling stained, but fortunately, Nylotte had been correct. Using the circle to meditate made that better, at least for a time. She layered her defenses, picturing the Atlantean in his glass box and putting walls around him. Stone, wood, force, fire, the layers went on one after the other, metaphysically blocking him from influencing her. *I don't need to know what he's up to right now. I need him locked away.*

After an hour, she was ready. She walked into the bunker's armory to find Idryll waiting for her. The space was rectangular, with Idryll's section to the right, Morrigan's to the left, and hers on the long wall, along with a couple of common cabinets. Their gear was on display, functional, and somewhat artistic. She'd read somewhere in the past that such touches helped warriors focus their minds and had been part of martial design since the Middle Ages. All she knew was that she felt clearer in purpose when she saw it all laid out like that. *Which is the same thing.*

Her partner sat cross-legged on the bench in front of her area, looking toward the center of the room. She said, "You ready for this?" Her normal bantering tone wasn't in evidence.

Ruby nodded. "Yeah. We're going to kick these bastards in the teeth and take my sister back. We'll find everyone else they've taken, too, once she's safe." Word had spread while she'd been tracking the Kilomea that a dozen people had been kidnapped and another four killed. "Hopefully we'll also get an idea of who's behind this. With Sloane dead, you'd think this garbage would've stopped."

Idryll shrugged. "You have something very valuable here in the city, and people will always want a piece of it. As long as you restrict access, you're going to have those willing to step across the line. It's how people work."

"Only those who follow a certain set of rules, or don't follow any rules. This is *our* place. They have so many others."

"Perhaps you should think about trying to share their space?"

Ruby shook her head. "I'm not sure if it's real or a mental feature on our part, but many magicals feel the need to have a clear foothold on this planet. The belief that what's ours is truly *ours*. While it started underground with the kemanas, that's no way to live long term." She ran her hand along her sword's scabbard, feeling the hard leather and thinking the weapon deserved something better. "Did Margrave come through with the stuff?"

Idryll nodded. "It's already in your gear. You're all set."

"Okay, then. Time to put it on." She thought Rath would appreciate her referencing *Men in Black* at this pivotal moment.

She donned the base layer of leather, which she'd thoroughly cleaned after her tumble from the bike. The tight material embraced her, increasing her focus. She snapped the collar closed at the neck and added the equipment belt at her waist. She touched each item on it automatically, verifying its presence. Her lightning grenades, Margrave's smoke, one of the new smaller model EMPs. A bulky cube sat at her lower back containing her small drone, and the controller for it went into a thigh pouch.

Next up was the bulletproof vest, which held two extra magazines for the pistol on her right thigh drop holster. It also carried a healing potion and an energy potion, backups for the ones in her left thigh pouch. Getting her sword strapped on over the vest was still a challenge, and she kept forgetting to ask Diana how she did it. When her hand touched the hilt to check the draw, the duo whispered in her mind. No castigations for once, only a feeling of support and unity of purpose. A sense of confidence spread from her core at the reassurance.

Next up were her shield bracelets, which held only two charges since she hadn't had time to refill them. The knockout dart launcher went above it on her right arm. Idryll had reloaded the darts, and she had four at her disposal. "Did you change the canister, too?"

Her partner clicked the fastener on her equipment belt and made a dismissive snort. "Of course. You can't go into battle with partial charges." She spoke as if she was instructing a child.

Ruby didn't mention her reduced bracelets as she returned to dressing. She laced up her boots, pulling them tight, and checked to make sure the throwing knives were still properly secured. Finally, she rested her hand on the hilt of her dagger and moved to face her companion. "How do I look?"

Idryll turned and raised an eyebrow. "Like you're ready to get our partner back."

Ruby nodded. "That I am. We only need one more tool." She activated her comm, which routed through the bunker's network. "Demetrius, you set up the thing with Alejo?"

The infomancer replied, "Hang on." A few seconds passed. Then he said, "Okay, saved what I was working on. What did you say?"

"Alejo."

"Right. She said the items you wanted will be next to the trophy and that she's spending the rest of the day out in the field. You know what that means?"

Ruby grinned at the amateur spycraft, which would nonetheless get the job done. "I do. We're good. Any word from Diana's people?"

"Kaylee and I have managed to crack into most of the cell networks. Another half-hour and we should be able to bring that fully online. One of them is driving around at random with the locator, but they haven't had a hit yet. Don't worry, we'll find her soon."

"I know you'll handle it perfectly." She deactivated the connection and said, "Okay, let's go to the portal room." They entered the space, which featured the finest unfinished drywall and laminate floor. No one could guess its location by seeing it through a portal, even if the lights were on, which they wouldn't be.

Ruby pulled the heavy door closed behind them and used force magic to reset each of the latches, one in the top, one into the floor, and three into the sides. It would be next to impossible for anyone who didn't know right where the latches were to disengage them with magic, and blasting the door would only succeed after a long period of concerted effort. Margrave had warded the thing to drain magic, and unless you knew where the gaps were, even accomplishing something as simple as undoing a latch would be seriously debilitating.

It did permit signals to escape, so if one of them found themselves trapped inside, they could call out with their comms. The final failsafe was an extra comm hidden behind the drywall. Ruby flicked on the light until the door was closed and latched, then turned it off again. She opened a portal to the sheriff's office and peered through to see that the woman had drawn her blinds and the space was dark. They stepped into the room, allowing the rift to close behind them. She pointed at the heavy backpacks on the couch. "Put that one on." She grabbed the other and did the same.

Idryll asked, "Are these what I think they are?"

She nodded. "Yeah. Supplied by the PDA, no less."

She laughed. "I'm guessing they don't know who they're for."

Ruby nodded. "Correct. They believe the sheriff's office needs them for some training."

"Why do we need these anchors, exactly?" Despite her complaints, the shapeshifter moved easily with the backpack on.

"Mainly because while there's no way to know what we'll face, the attackers this time included magicals. We have an edge with our combat abilities and equipment in any straight-up fight, so if we find ourselves in trouble, we trigger these anti-magic things to shift the playing field in our favor."

Idryll nodded. "Sensible plan. You came up with it?"

Ruby laughed. She couldn't help it. "Don't sound so incredulous. I'm not an idiot all the time, despite your belief that I am."

Her partner grinned, showing her teeth. "You're learning, and that's all to the good. Let's go get our teammate."

CHAPTER TWENTY-SIX

A series of portals had taken them to a three-story structure out in the middle of nowhere, near Reno. They'd stopped partway so Ruby could remove the locators the PDA had hidden inside the backpacks. Margrave had given her the tech to detect them. Kaylee and Demetrius had finally managed to access enough towers that they were able to get a faint hint of Morrigan's location, and their roving tracker got closer to confirm it. Ruby took the device from the agent and secured it to her belt, offered her thanks, and focused on the building ahead.

In her ear, Demetrius said, "Feed coming now." One of her eyepieces blurred, then displayed the image from the drone flying at maximum height above the installation. They'd figured the place would have good security and didn't want to risk discovery any earlier than necessary. Her greatest concern was that the enemy would respond to an incursion by killing all the captives. She couldn't see a way that was profitable, not given the roster of people they'd taken. *All children of or partners of casino owners. You don't throw away that kind of leverage without thinking about it a few times first.* Since she wasn't inside the head of whoever was behind it, the worry stayed.

They hadn't managed to get that information out of the Kilomea. She had her suspicions, since it was Reno, that it might have something to do with Sloane's organization. However, as Demetrius had pointed out, lots of people lived in Reno, and that connection was maybe a bit of a reach based on the evidence at hand. *Still, I'm going to find out who worked with him as soon as we finish with this. Just in case.*

The drone showed a square complex centered on the building. Only one road provided access, and the same heavy chain-link fence topped with razor wire that ran along the perimeter of the place blocked it. The buzz and pull of static told them the barrier was electrified from ten feet away. Idryll observed, "That's pretty serious."

"What do you know about electrical fences?"

The shapeshifter replied, "Enough that I don't want to mess with that one, that's for sure."

Ruby shook her head without taking her eyes off the space beyond the fence Idryll didn't want to mess with. "Tree, any sign of technological or magical alarms inside the perimeter?"

"None that the drone can detect. Which, you know, is pretty concerning in itself."

"Yeah. Agreed." The place wouldn't be unguarded, which meant the tricks and traps that awaited them were of the sophisticated variety if the drone couldn't spot them. *Fine, whatever.* She killed the connection to her boyfriend and turned to Idryll. "Okay. We're going to go up and over the fence. I need you to stay close because the steps behind us will vanish. I'm trying to keep my magical emanations concealed here." Nonetheless, she wrapped herself in force magic and did the same with her companion. While she couldn't maintain both shields during any significant confusion, she had enough brainpower to manage it for a while, as long as no one was actively working to kill them.

She created stairs out of force magic and stepped up, with Idryll right behind her. Soon they were stepping carefully down on the opposite side of the fence and crouching to avoid setting off any sound or motion sensors that might be nearby. The tech goggles flicked through detection modes as she ran her gaze systematically over the ground ahead, again finding nothing. She muttered, "My best guess is physical dangers hidden by magic, although I suppose there could be magic with technological triggers. In any case, keep an eye out for tripwires, lasers, pressure pads, that sort of thing. Hell, watch out for landmines. Who knows how serious these bastards are about security?"

As they made their way ever so slowly toward the building, staying low, crawling in places to remain invisible in the dust and shrubs, they came across several of each kind, except the landmines. Ruby had brought along toys to counteract everything she could think of and had parted with a third of her stockpile before they spotted the next challenge. Idryll hissed, and Ruby froze. "What?"

Her partner replied, "Go to thermal, look ahead and to the right."

Hidden in a bush that might've been artificially constructed for the purpose was a figure, seated but with arms extended as though holding the handles of a weapon. "Nice catch."

"Want me to take him out?"

Ruby shook her head. "The chances are excellent that they have a radio routine set up and will notice if he's missing. No. The presence of humans on the outside makes me think magicals on the inside are the real threat. These are mainly to discourage any general challenge that might arise. It also explains why we haven't found any magical traps out here. Like on the Strip, they're using the humans basically as chasers, with magicals as the hammer. Let's slip past."

She reinforced the veils they'd been traveling under, and they snuck carefully in between two of the positions, which were rather obvious once they knew what to look for. They found some protective shrubbery twenty feet from the building, and Ruby gazed up at it. "Well, it's basically a cement blockhouse. Awesome. Great design, Reno. Really attractive stuff. Demetrius, have you figured out what this place was?"

She wouldn't have risked using the radio if not for the encrypted booster on her belt, specifically designed to control signal leak. It used line-of-sight to a repeater she'd placed beyond the perimeter. He replied, "Private company, definitely just a shell. If I had to guess, based upon what I've seen so far, this looks like a government thing. CIA, FBI, something."

She scowled. "You don't think it's them *now*, do you?"

"No. Seems as if this place went dormant in the records decades ago. I'm guessing someone bought it or is borrowing it."

The news inspired some relief. While she'd fight through whatever she had to in order to free her sister, not winding up in the crosshairs of the government was an outcome to be desired. She pulled the drone from the case on her belt and hit the button to unfold it, then used the controller to fly it around the building. It made a complete circuit, and by the end, they'd only found a garage with multiple bays and a single entrance door on the opposite side. "Damn, these people were serious about security."

She slid her fingers across the device to make the drone climb to get a look at the roof. Amidst the rooftop heating and cooling equipment was an access door. The building had no windows at all, and she would bet that its construction was a continuous pour of concrete into a frame, meant to be invulnerable. *This sort of place should contain the Hulk, not my sister. Although it's true, she's not much fun when she's angry, either.*

She landed the drone on the roof and paused with her finger hovering over the destruct button, waiting to see if it triggered any alarms. After five minutes without a reaction, she felt fairly confident they were still undiscovered. She was pretty sure she'd plotted out all the cameras at the beginning, and hadn't seen any up there, so that wasn't an entirely unexpected development. Ruby went up to the building, strengthened her veil, and said, "Wait here," to Idryll, who immediately knelt in the shadows.

Ruby blasted herself to the top with force magic, landing softly on the edge, not wanting to go any further before taking a good solid look at the surface. Turning, she let a line of force fall from her hand, then braced herself as

Idryll climbed up it in a quick crawl. She muttered, "Damn, you're heavy."

Idryll laughed. "No, you're weak. Also, it should be me taking risks like that, not you."

Ruby shook her head. "Whatever. Let's get moving." She crouched and peered carefully over the tar and gravel surface, trying to spot any obvious locations where traps might be waiting. She couldn't find any and hoped that whoever was using the place hadn't had time to outfit the area with magic detection. This high up, probably they'd count on the humans outside as the main deterrent and focus most of the magical defenses inside the building. She layered force steps again so they didn't have to walk on the surface, and they crossed to the door. Naturally, it was locked. Ruby crouched and pulled a tool from her belt, setting it to the lock.

Idryll commented, "That's new. What is it?"

A *click* signaled success, and Ruby put the device away with a satisfied grin. "Electronic lock breaker. Diana's folks gave it to me. They really do have the best toys. I need to get Kayleigh and Margrave together sometime."

Her companion laughed. "They'd never stop talking. Then they'd probably both die of hunger because they'd forget to eat while they were working."

She nodded. "Good point. Put that one on the back burner. For now, let's go find whoever's holding my sister and beat them into rubble."

CHAPTER TWENTY-SEVEN

They descended the stairwell cautiously, pausing after each step to survey the surfaces ahead for traps, physical or magical. None was apparent, and the door at the bottom that led onto the third floor was unlocked. Ruby listened carefully for any sign of life beyond the barrier but found none. She checked the tracker, which showed Morrigan closer to the other side of the building. "Okay, here we go." She called up her full-body force shield, wrapped one around Idryll, put another in front of them, and used her magic to open the door.

No response came, so she swung the door all the way open and moved through it, letting the largest shield fall. The area was dark, lit only by small circles in the ceiling that did little to alleviate the gloom. Her magical mask's technological eyepieces shifted to lowlight mode, rendering everything in a greenish haze. The hallway was wider than normal, reminding her of a hospital corridor big enough to push a stretcher through.

She led Idryll forward, and they opened the doors to

either side as they progressed. The left side of the hallway had more of them, each revealing a small enclosure that looked very much like cells. The opposite wall's doors gave access to larger rooms, with chairs resembling ones she'd seen at her dentist's office bolted to the floor.

Idryll asked, "Torture chambers?"

The same thought had occurred to Ruby. "Or medical bays. Maybe this was a hospital."

Her partner shook her head. "Doesn't *feel* like a hospital."

"Yeah. I hear that."

Morrigan's cell was at the far end of the dozen on the left side of the hallway. Ruby yanked open the door, only to find the chamber empty. Disappointment cascaded over her. She growled, "I knew we couldn't get that lucky. This thing only works in two dimensions, so she must be on one of the lower levels."

Idryll nodded. "Makes sense, since this floor doesn't have actual power or anything."

"It has defenses, though." Ruby pointed up at the cameras and the gates set into the walls that presumably could spring shut at need.

"Wonder why they aren't active."

She shrugged. "Old building, maybe the electricity is inoperative on this level."

Idryll frowned back at the door they'd come through. "Or they wanted to provide an easy entrance on the top floor to persuade any invader to select that route."

"Well, if that was their plan, they succeeded."

"Should we activate the backpacks?"

The mention inspired Ruby to shrug hers up to

recenter the weight. "No. Those are our emergency back-ups. We don't use them until there's a real need." She pointed ahead. "Another staircase. Makes sense from a security perspective that each flight only goes down a level. Hopefully, we'll find Morrigan on the next floor."

Idryll nodded. "Hopefully there's not a basement."

"Thanks for that happy thought." Ruby used force magic to open the door barely far enough to peer through. The stairway was dark, but her eyepiece display came alive with a chaotic arrangement of beams and sensors. She breathed, "Wow. That's unwelcoming."

Idryll peered through the doorway below her. "Both technology and magic?"

She replied, "Yep. Total maze. Everything set up kind of haphazardly, like portable units that someone stuck down at random. I don't see a way to get through without tripping them. So, I guess we'll need to go loud earlier than we'd hoped." She worried, again, that the kidnappers might respond violently to cut their losses and escape.

Idryll said, "There's another option."

Ruby frowned. "What?"

"I can make it through there in my smallest form."

She refused automatically. "You'd be going in without anything. That would be plain stupid."

Her companion shook her head and slid out of the backpack's straps. "In the stairwell, all I need is to be small and agile. On the floor below, teeth and claws will suffice." The resolve in her voice was unmistakable. It was clear her partner intended to do it with or without Ruby's blessing. *Dammit.*

She sighed. "Okay. Be careful. Once you get Morrigan

out, tell her to go home, then you and I can finish finding the others."

"Will do." Idryll shrank to the size of a large house cat and slipped through the opening, headed for the floor below.

In this form, Idryll sensed more than saw the traps along the way as she crawled and jumped to avoid them. She'd created a mental map while looking through her lenses and remembered the path easily. The scents of the building were plentiful but mostly annoying. Dust, unwashed humans, several varieties of magicals. The second floor was active, filled with noises made by people moving about and murmuring, and on what she judged to be the other end of the level, an argument of some kind.

She pressed up against the door leading from the stairwell and shifted back into her normal form to insert a claw against the adhesive edge of the alarm sensor on the frame, detaching it so it wouldn't lose contact when the door moved. She opened it and slipped through, already returned to her feline form before it closed softly behind her. From this angle, the cells were on the right, the larger rooms on the left. The hallway seemed gargantuan in her smaller form.

On this level, the doors along the right side had indicator lights, all of which she could see glowing. *Presumably locked. So how does one unlock them?* She noticed the doors in the left-hand wall were set differently from the floor above, an additional entrance visible in the line nearest to her current position. *If I were putting in a security office, that would be a good place for it. Especially if they weren't thinking about someone coming in from the roof.*

That door had no indicator and stood slightly ajar. She poked her nose into it and found a control desk directly in front of her. It looked like something from an old spy movie or war film, huge and grey, with lots of screens. Behind it was a man in a black leather jacket and dirty jeans, his heavy boots propped up on the station. His head bounced in rhythm with whatever he heard through his tiny earbuds. To her ears, it sounded tinny and awful, but he seemed to enjoy it.

Idryll crouched and scuttled behind him on soft paws, then rose to her humanoid form and put him in a choke-hold. He feebly thrashed as she cut off the blood flow to his brain, then passed out. She lowered him gently to the floor, making sure both he and his chair landed with a minimum of noise. She considered kicking him in the temple to ensure he stayed out but knew Ruby wouldn't want her to risk killing him with the blow. *Trash like this doesn't deserve to live.*

Nonetheless, she left him lying there and turned to the control panel. Two rows of buttons, each matching the number of cells on the second floor and presumably the first, were positioned under stacked lights that glowed red. She pressed the one that should correspond to Morrigan's cell, and the indicator switched to green. Her speed wasn't quite a run to reach the door, but it was definitely more than a walk. She opened it and caught Morrigan's fist as it flew out at her. "Whoa, easy there."

Ruby's sister offered a thin smile. She looked haggard,

equal parts tired and worried, with maybe a little fear mixed in. "Idryll. Thank goodness. We have to get the others. Our captors let slip that there's a bunch of us here."

Idryll, who had turned at a noise from further down the hallway, replied, "I think we have a bigger problem."

Morrigan growled, "Oh, good. Ever since they took me, I've been dreaming of payback. The Kilomea is mine." She charged, and Idryll followed with a roar.

CHAPTER TWENTY-EIGHT

Morrigan hadn't enjoyed her recent past. She'd woken in a cell with a splitting headache, immediately and thoroughly furious with herself for not seeing the attack coming. *At the very least, I should've had some defenses up as a precaution.* Sometimes, managing the different roles of civilian and fighter was a challenge, but in the future, she planned to err on the side of the latter. *So what if people think Morrigan Achera is tough? Maybe what I need is a new image.*

Those thoughts filtered through her mind as she closed the distance to the Kilomea. She wasn't sure if he was the person who'd hit her or if he'd even been there. Still, she had a score to settle, and since he was part of the group holding her captive, he was fair game. *If he was one of the three, so much the better.* Idryll flashed past, faster on her feet, and effectively interposed herself between anyone else who might've gotten involved with Morrigan and her target. *Thanks, partner.*

The Kilomea whipped a punch at head level, right where she would've been if she hadn't stopped her headlong charge a moment before in anticipation of such a move. The swing didn't open him up as much as she'd hoped, but she managed an elbow smash into his ribs before she had to dart backward to avoid a jab from his other fist. He growled, more in annoyance than pain, it appeared. She'd struck something resistant, and part of her mind noted that she'd have to hit more vulnerable spots since he was wearing armor. *Fine, whatever.*

He snarled, "Get back in your cell, little girl, and perhaps you can avoid getting hurt."

"Pain doesn't concern me. All I care about is seeing you bleeding on the floor and begging for mercy."

He set his feet in an even stance, ready to shift in any needed direction. "You will have a long wait if that's your desire."

"We'll see." She took a step forward and jumped, raising both of her knees to her chest and slamming her heels out at him. He lifted his arms to block, taking the shot on padded forearms, and she fell to her back. He moved in, thinking her vulnerable, exactly as she'd hoped. She shouted in anger and lashed out with force magic, blasting a bolt into each of his knees. The right one was bent when the magic struck, and it twisted sideways, probably tearing something inside. His left one, though, was locked out when the bolt hit.

The joint broke with a loud *snap*, and he fell to the floor, clutching it. She bounced up and stood over him, then pulled back her foot and started kicking any areas his hands weren't protecting. Eventually, he was moaning and covering his face while she landed blows to his torso. She'd left her impractical shoes behind in the cell, and the soreness in her feet finally convinced her to stop attacking. She knelt beside him and said, "That's only the start. If you're still here when I finish with the rest of your people, we're going to continue this. You might want to start crawling."

While her partner took on the single giant, Idryll threw herself at the other four people in the corridor. They all wore leather jackets like the first and the same dirty jeans and heavy boots. They went straight for magic though, doubtless realizing they couldn't stand against her in a purely physical contest. She dove aside from an electrical blast, thankful for the wide hallway, and leapt over the line of fire that scored the tile seeking her.

Her dodges carried her into the middle of them, forcing the nearest pair to turn their wands into force blades to slash at her instead of risking hitting their comrades with ranged attacks. She leaned aside from the initial blow and pivoted to avoid the second. They were good, or at least good for wizards who didn't spend much time training. However, they lacked armor to protect them, so when she extended her claws and slashed them, her foes wound up bloody. The first stumbled back in disbelief at the set of four deep cuts running down his chest, and she stabbed the other through the wand arm, forcing fingers that suddenly wouldn't work to drop the implement. She spun into a kick that caught him in the head and took him out.

The move opened the firing lines for the other pair. She dove and rolled right before lightning cascaded over where she'd stood. A few thin tendrils snapped and buzzed near her but didn't connect. She didn't give the other one time to bring his fire beam in line but charged the one who'd hit her, ramming both sets of claws straight into his throat. He fell, beyond saving, and the scene shocked the other enough that she was able to skip into a sidekick and bounce the side of his head off a nearby wall. She punched him to make sure he wouldn't get back up again, then turned to look for more trouble.

None materialized, but it was clear that they had now "gone loud." Idryll said, "Ruby wants you to portal to safety."

Morrigan growled, "No chance. We have to get down-stairs and rescue the rest."

She nodded. "Somehow I knew you'd say that."

Neither humor nor mercy colored Morrigan's tone. "Let's get to it before something bad happens."

"I'll go unlock all the cells. Hang on a minute."

At first, only silence came from below, then a couple of minutes later, the sound of fighting wafted up the stairs. Ruby growled inwardly at the realization that at least Idryll, and probably Idryll and her sister, weren't going to adhere to the plan she'd laid out. She muttered, "Idiots. Predictable. You suck."

She paced momentarily, wondering how to deal with the traps in the stairwell, and shrugged. "If there's no need for secrecy, there's no need for subtlety." Entering one of the rooms that might have been medical labs or might have been torture chambers, she used a blast of force to break the chair free of its moorings. She levitated it to the stairwell, yanked open the door, and threw it bouncing down the stairs to set off all the traps along the way. The chair from the other room repeated the process to ensure she'd triggered them all, and she rushed down the steps.

The others were about to enter the stairs leading to the first floor when she caught up to them. "You couldn't listen, for once?"

Idryll shook her head. "I tried, really."

Ruby nodded. "Oh, I'm *so* sure that you did. Probably worked *really* hard to convince her."

Her sister's pallor was concerning, and the look on her face promised violence to come. Morrigan snapped, "Less talking, more freeing prisoners."

"Are you sure you won't go back to where it's safe? You don't even have any equipment."

"I have my magic. That's all I need."

While they'd been conversing, Idryll had secured her equipment belt and donned the backpack Ruby had brought along. The tiger-woman said, "If she stays at the back and attacks from surprise she'll be fine."

Ruby recalled the strategy from the second run with the agents and nodded. "Okay. It's your call." She opened the door and spotted another set of traps, then closed it again. "Hang on. I need to borrow a chair."

CHAPTER TWENTY-NINE

When the smoke cleared, they pelted down the steps. Morrigan said, "It didn't seem like these people are the ones running the show. They're hirelings. So they probably have a solid reason not to hurt any of the captives."

Ruby replied, "Good to know. Give me a sec." She unpacked the small drone again and got it flying. "Okay, open the door a little." She sent the tiny aircraft swinging through the gap, and it lasted all of three seconds before the feed vanished in the brilliance of a fireball. "Bastards. I spent a lot of time building that. Clearly, they're aware we made it this far."

She inhaled a centering breath. "Okay, here's what we're going to do, and no arguing. Idryll and I rush forward and engage whoever's there. Morrigan, you open the doors and portal people to the receiving room at the abbey. Abbott Thomas is aware that he might have visitors." She peeled off her stun knuckles and handed them to her sister. "They're fully charged and can be recharged with lightning. Now, veil up." She cast her illusion, layering it over her force shield, and concealed Idryll as well. Morrigan vanished as she applied her disguise. "Let's do it."

Ruby ripped open the door, summoned a force shield in front of her, and charged into the hallway. Their enemies had organized themselves into two disparate groups. Nearer were several Atlanteans: dark-haired, dark-skinned, and to judge by the looks on their faces, dark-tempered. She shuddered as the artifact pulsed and twisted in her flesh, apparently recognizing its brethren. She reached back and drew her sword, needing the support of the pair inside, and grabbed her dagger with her other hand.

By the time the first blasts came her way, she had dodged aside and held up her knife to anchor a force barrier. It caught everything but the lightning that cascaded around her, chewing at her full-body shield. She shouted, "Kagji," to reinforce it with her pendant. Realizing that the incoming magical barrage was too much for her to handle and still make any progress, she threw her dagger at the nearest foe and transferred the sword to her left hand.

The artifact took advantage of the instant where she wasn't in contact with the weapon to send a wave of queasiness through her, almost causing her to fumble it. She sent fury spiraling inward, pushing away the discomfort and imagining the energy battering her unwanted passenger. It was on a rising tide of anger that she drew her pistol, and it was that rage that caused her to aim for center mass without even considering trying to wound her opponents.

Two squeezes of the trigger for each to start, and when the weapon *clicked* empty, all the Atlanteans were on the floor, bleeding. She calmly ejected the magazine and let it drop, then awkwardly shifted the pistol into her left hand along with the sword, pulled out a magazine from her vest, and slotted it in place. Racking the slide was equally difficult, but when she re-holstered the gun, it was ready to shoot. She spared a single glance for the seriously wounded individuals on the linoleum floor and shook her head. "You don't go after kids and families. What the hell's wrong with you people?"

She felt a disturbing lack of remorse as she strode forward to assist her partner.

Idryll had charged past Ruby en route to the second set of enemies. She noted that the hallway seemed shorter than the last, and ended in a larger door, then shunted those thoughts aside as she flowed into the middle of the group of women awaiting her. Several of them had drawn wands and blasted at her on the way in, but her natural agility had been more than equal to the task of dodging the attacks, and concern over hitting the others had limited their fire.

Fortunately, Idryll wasn't limited at all. She punched the first woman she came to, an elf who blocked with a crisp strike and countered with a punch to Idryll's ribs. She bent away enough to blunt the impact, then kicked out with her right leg, slamming her shin into the other woman's. Idryll had a lot of experience with the pain that a shin blow caused and had prepared for it. Her opponent wasn't and sagged to the ground, screaming at the agony that coursed through her. Idryll dipped down and landed a shot to the woman's face that banged her head off the floor, and she was no longer a concern.

While she was down, flame washed over her and her opponent. Her anti-magic deflector drank it in and cracked, but it had given her the time she needed to lurch into motion again. The witch that had cast it was off to her left, and Idryll slammed a kick into her stomach. Despite the force shield the woman summoned, the impact knocked her backward and gave Idryll enough distance to leap and smash an elbow into her face. That one went down, too.

Pain ripped through her arm as daggers of ice slashed into her flesh, and she dropped and rolled away from them. When she came up, it was as a tiger, and her paws tore gouges into the floor as she hurtled forward to ram bodily into the witch who had attacked her and who could marshal nothing more than a scream in her defense. The other woman went flying, and Idryll whipped her claws out at the next closest, severing her hamstring and dropping her.

The final one cast a force shield around herself. Idryll leapt, wrapped her paws around the woman's shoulders, and drove her strong jaws in at her throat. The witch went down from the impact, her shield collapsing until it lay right outside her skin, the teeth an inch away from her neck. She gasped, "I yield." Idryll opened her mouth a little and gave a quick nod. Her foe threw her wand aside, and the protective barrier vanished. She considered tearing her foe's throat out anyway, but a deal was a deal. Instead, she head-butted the woman, knocking her senseless, and turned to look for more enemies.

While her teammates were fighting, Morrigan moved quickly from cell to cell, opening the doors and summoning portals to send the occupants to the abbey. She got a surprise in the middle when she opened the door, and an elf who'd hidden inside stabbed at her throat with a dagger. Her keyed-up reflexes were as high as they'd ever been though, and she blocked the blow and delivered an uppercut with the knuckles that *snapped* loudly and dropped him to the floor. *Even without the shock, he would've been out from that shot. Serves you right, jerk.*

She grabbed the blade and went to stick it in her belt, remembered she wasn't wearing one and threw it away in disgust. "When I find out who's behind all this, we're going to have a nice long talk that involves many breaking bones and probably a lot of screaming." The image amused her as she cleared the rest of the cells, then met up with Ruby and Idryll.

Her sister went down the list of missing people, and Morrigan checked them off one by one against those she'd sent through the portal. When they finished the list, two remained unrescued—twins, children of the Drow who owned Darkest Night. Ruby said, "Okay. They have to be behind that door, and if I have my map right, that's the garage."

Idryll nodded. "I concur."

Morrigan knew the words were coming before they arrived, and still, she couldn't think of an argument against them. Her sister said, "Mo, you have to go. It's sure to be some sort of trap, and you don't have any gear with you.

Trust me. We're all set. Head to the abbey and help our people get back where they belong."

Tears welled in her eyes. Maybe at the realization that she was about to be safe for the first time since the ordeal began, or in gratitude to her sister and Idryll. Or maybe in frustration that she would miss out on whatever was behind the door. Still, she knew she'd be a liability, and while she would've taken the risk for herself, she couldn't endanger the other two that way. She nodded and sniffed. "See you after. Be careful."

Ruby grinned. "You know it."

They headed for the garage, and Morrigan didn't look back as she summoned a portal and hopped through to the safety of the abbey.

CHAPTER THIRTY

They entered the garage and discovered the Drow kids inside, cowering at the opposite end of the space. The area was as wide as the entire building, but probably only about twenty feet deep, enough for two large cars end-to-end without too much room left over. No vehicles were present, only six Dark Elves in addition to the captives. One stepped forward, a woman with a white crewcut, battle leathers, dual swords, and knives. She said neutrally, "I presume you freed the others?"

Ruby nodded. "You have this single opportunity to surrender. Not all of your friends survived, and I can't promise you will, either."

She snorted. "Not my friends and their fate is irrelevant. You stand no chance of defeating us, no matter how good you are. All you did was make our negotiating position that much better."

Idryll said, "With whoever hired you."

The Drow inclined her head. "If you wish to believe it so."

Ruby growled, "Last chance."

The other woman countered, "Last chance for you to escape with your lives."

"Pop the packs and hit them." Ruby yanked the lanyard that activated the anti-magic emitter in her backpack and charged forward, drawing her pistol as she went. The leader stepped back, and the others closed ranks in front of her. She heard the *hum* of Idryll's pack activating and almost laughed at the shocked look on the Dark Elves' faces when they tried to throw magic but couldn't.

Ruby aimed her gun at the nearest, only to have it knocked from her grasp by an expertly thrown dagger that sliced along her hand. She shouted, "Ow," and wished she had one of Margrave's conceptual skin-absorbent-healing-packs at her disposal. Instead, she reached over her shoulder and grabbed her sword with the slick hand, squeezing it tightly and hoping the wound wasn't as deep as it was painful.

Their foes reacted admirably to losing their magical advantage, drawing their preferred weapons and surging to meet them. Two came at Ruby and three went for Idryll, apparently finding her claws the greater threat. *Well, now I'm insulted.* The pair bracing her moved so she couldn't hit them both with a single strike, and she stayed in motion to prevent them from surrounding her. One held daggers, and they licked out quickly and repeatedly, seeking an opening. She evaded them with quick steps and blocked them with her shield bracelets, trusting the metal cuffs to keep her from damage while she used her sword against the Drow holding a matching weapon.

Even with the anti-magic emitters running, Shalia and

Tyrsh spoke into her mind, glorying in the battle. Making subtle shifts in accord with their suggestions got her inside the man's guard. She slammed her hilt into his nose, and when he staggered backward, slashed down in a diagonal, opening a deep cut across his chest. He fell as blood flowed from the wound. She turned to the other. "Not much without your magic, are you?"

He threw a knife at her face in response. She blocked it and strode in, intent on ending him quickly and getting to the kids.

Idryll didn't like the three-on-one odds at all and was determined to improve them immediately. She charged at the closest foe, arriving as he got his daggers properly seated in his grasp. She stabbed out, twisting her wrists, and her claws buried themselves in his upper arms. They tore down the length of the limbs, opening veins and sending him screaming to the ground. She took a painful but not particularly damaging kick to the side from a nearby enemy and swiped her claws at his leg, but he retracted it quickly enough to avoid damage.

Now that it was two on one, she circled with the pair, meeting feints from the daggers with swipes of her claws and evading blows from the longer sword. They said words, but she was deep in her predator's mind, and the sounds they made were nothing but the bleating of prey. She twitched at the sword wielder, and the one with the knives took the opportunity to strike, as she'd hoped.

Idryll sidestepped and delivered a kick to his chest, then

put the foot down and pivoted, bringing her other one up in a sweeping kick to his groin. Her foe doubled over, and she landed a punch to the back of his neck, sheathing her claws in a momentary act of mercy. He went face-first into the garage's concrete floor, and she turned to engage the third. That opponent looked far less confident now than he had when she was outnumbered and angled his sword in a defensive stance. She grinned, showing her fangs. "Poor little elf. Now you're all alone."

Ruby finished off the one with the daggers quickly, a stab through an arm rendering it useless, followed by a quick kick that broke his leg. She snapped his other wrist to be sure he couldn't easily reenter the fight and punched him in the temple before heading for the Drow leader. She looked at Ruby and shook her head slowly, backing as far away as she could. "Nice play, can't argue with that."

Ruby scowled. "Shut the hell up, hand over the kids, and lay down on your face with your hands behind your head. I'm only going to ask once."

The Dark Elf laughed. "You think you've won, but you have to remember. We're on *my* home turf." She hit a button, and one of a pair of innocuous old crates located at the back corners of the garage fell open with a pop to reveal a machine gun turret. The Drow finished, "Which means I have toys you haven't even thought about."

Before her foe could trigger the gun, Ruby grabbed the EMP Margrave had created and threw it at the turret. Only afterward did she remember the device required lightning to activate. She shouted, "Kill the bags," and yanked on the lanyard. When she felt her power return, she blasted the thing with lightning, and the turret whirred to a stop without firing a single round.

However, the crate on the other side of the garage had already opened to reveal another. She had to call up a force shield to protect against it and summon a second in front of Idryll. The devices looked old, and she could only duck and hope the Dark Elves hadn't loaded them with anti-magic bullets. The Drow had prepared the battleground well, and as the thing started to spit out rounds that deflected from her shield, Ruby realized the barrage was too strong for her to do anything but defend. Her enemy summoned a portal, pushed the kids through, and gave a saucy wave before departing.

When the bullets finally ran out, Ruby let out a string of curses, screaming them at the ceiling. When she'd finished, Idryll asked, "Feel better?"

"No. Shut up." She used a force blast to create a hole in the garage door and stalked outside, but her minuscule hope that the Drow would've been trying to get outside turned out to be as whimsical as she'd imagined it would be. They'd saved most, but not all. The fury that inspired was all hers, no hint of the artifact tainting it.

Idryll touched her shoulder tentatively, then gripped it harder. "This is a win. We'll get the others back."

Ruby nodded and put her hand over the shapeshifter's. "Damn right we will."

CHAPTER THIRTY-ONE

Julianna Sloane rode in the back of the armored SUV, trying and failing to get rid of her scowl. Her lieutenants sat across from her, looking equally upset. She said, "Who was captured?"

Smith replied, "Three of the meeting attendees. Don't worry. They won't talk."

"Who has them?"

Thompson said, "PDA."

Julianna gritted her teeth. "Do we have people in that organization?"

Smith was almost apologetic. "Only low-level."

She shook her head. "Anyone with direct knowledge of our involvement has to be freed or killed immediately. I don't care which, and I don't care how. This *can't* be allowed to connect back to us. Do you understand?"

Her lieutenants blinked, seeming surprised at her ruthless demand, then nodded. The SUV slowed to a stop, and the sound of a garage door closing came through the vehicle's skin. Smith climbed out and offered her a hand.

She took it and walked from the garage into the living room of a suburban home. Inside the door was a hard-looking Drow male holding a pistol in his right hand and doubtless with a spell ready to cast. When he recognized them, he stepped aside with a nod.

She continued onward to find the Drow bounty hunter, the only one who had succeeded at her task, reclined in the living room. Her feet were up on the coffee table as she watched a screen showing two children playing in what looked like a bedroom. Blocks floated in the air between the pair, with Xs and Os on them, and she realized they were using magic to play tic-tac-toe. *I guess that makes sense, learning through games.*

She shifted her gaze to the Dark Elf. "Are they well?"

The other woman nodded. "Very. A little put off by the fighting, as you might expect, but they're rebounding adequately."

"Are you ready for the next phase?"

The Drow laughed and dropped her feet to the floor, leaning forward. "Just tell me which finger you want to send."

Julianna released a dark chuckle. "Hopefully that won't be necessary. Very good work. There will be a bonus payment in your account by the end of the day." She turned to her lieutenants. "Thompson, begin Phase Two of this operation. Smith, find us more competent people for the next round of attacks. Those Magic City bastards haven't begun to suffer."

Ruby's body was in her meditation space, kneeling on the hard floor with magical wards raised around her. Her mind though, was in a place of her creation. Oddly enough, it took the form of a comfortable living room set in the middle of a wide-open grassland. The sun shone overhead, the only clouds in the sky were aesthetically pleasing, and a trio of chairs rested on an ornamental rug facing one another in a triangle.

Shalia sat to her left, and Tyrsh was on her right. Her sword's personalities seemed quite satisfied with the most recent battle and had congratulated her on her previous wise choice to use them against the artifact.

She asked, "Can you do anything more to help me with it?"

They looked uncomfortably at one another, then Shalia shook her head. "We've given you all the support we're able. Short of having us constantly at hand, where we are empowered to provide active assistance, you have the best we can offer."

Ruby sighed. "In that case, my options seem seriously limited. Meditation works, but that requires finding the time to do so. As recent events have shown, that's not always practical." She shook her head as the realization of what she had to do descended upon her. *Nadar is going to be so happy.* "I guess my only option is to see if completing the next stage of the *venamisha* will give me something that I can use against it. More power, a tool, anything."

The two looked reluctant, but they nodded in agreement. "Be sure to bring us along, and use us wisely."

Ruby smiled. "Wouldn't have it any other way."

Her body opened its eyes, and she rose stiffly to her feet. "How long was I out?"

From beyond the locked door, Idryll's muffled voice replied, "Two hours."

She sighed. *Time is so not on my side.* "Okay, open up."

Morrigan said, "First we have to make sure it's you. Tell me what happened when we went to that fancy restaurant for Dad's birthday when you were twelve."

She groaned. "Seriously?"

"We're only being careful, as Diana told you we should be."

Ruby rolled her eyes. "I spilled lobster bisque all over myself, and Dralen called me crusty crustacean for a week."

Both Morrigan and Idryll were laughing as the door opened. Ruby said crossly, "You know, the artifact will probably have access to my memories if it wins."

Her sister nodded. "I know. I just love hearing that story."

Ruby smacked her sibling as Idryll laughed. The shapeshifter said, "So, what's the plan?"

"There's only one thing I can think of. We're heading back to Oriceran to fulfill the next part of the prophecy."

Idryll stared her hard in the eyes. "You're taking me with you. Any argument and I'll kill you right now."

Ruby smiled in genuine affection for her partner's loyalty. "I wouldn't have it any other way."

THE STORY CONTINUES

Challenges continue to present themselves to Ruby as the bad guys just can't get the message: Don't mess with Magic City! Continue Ruby's adventures with Idryll and her team in *Law and Disorder in Magic City*.

Thank you for reading Book 5 in the Magic City Chronicles, and for continuing on to read these author notes! This was a tough one, not going to lie. But it sets up the three-book finish really well, and I believe stands alone as strongly as any of the others.

Another one of those surprise moments was the appearance of the Drow in the alley. I had planned for the gang members to go after human tourists, and then he showed up out of nowhere. I love it when that happens, even though it means extra revision and planning to make it work.

Did you ever wonder why the Drow are so often villains, historically speaking, in fantasy? I mean, until Drizzt, I don't think there was a non-bad-person Dark Elf in the genre. My argument would be that a difficult life underground has made them all highly capable, and they bring that capability to the surface, where it looks like something different.

I'm really interested to see what our new addition to Magic City turns out to be!

Martha has given her blessing to the idea of bringing back the Federal Agents of Magic (FAM) for my next series. Tentatively, it'll be Rogue Agents of Magic (RAM) which I think works really well. It's my plan that, just like Diana, Rath, and company have appeared in the Scions and Magic City series, we'll see Ruby, Idryll, Cali, and Fyre in that series. I can't wait to see what everyone has been up to while we've been spending our time in Magic City!

Civilization VI is beyond addictive. No one should play it. Next up is Sackboy on the PS5, I think. I still have to finish The Last of Us 2, but it went into a flashback and I lost interest and then I bought Civilization and it keeps crashing.... Oh, the trials and tribulations of being me. So challenging. <eyeroll>

WandaVision is perhaps the most unique show I've ever watched. It's good. Quite good. But I can't really binge it or anything. The Falcon and the Winter Soldier, on the other hand, it hitting all the right notes for me. Started on Star Trek: Discovery as well, and I have to say, the first season really holds up against the best of Trek.

The kid is pumped for the Marvel movies in the theatres this year. So am I. We made our pilgrimage to Hershey Park for opening day, which is an experience we'll (hopefully) never do again. Amusement parks and cold weather just don't go together.

I'm working on an epic amusement park trip for the summer. Three parks, plus a half-day hike in a giant cave, a full day of hiking in a waterfall-filled state park, and finish with a visit to my longest-lasting friend. Then, maybe one more Amusement park on the way home. I'm not sure I have the stamina to keep up with a 10-year-old for that long one on one, though. I'm not sure anyone does.

Before I go, once again, if this series is your first taste of my Urban Fantasy, look for "Magic Ops." I promise you'll enjoy it, and you'll get more of Diana, Rath, and company. You might also enjoy my science fiction work. All my writing is filled with action, snark, and villains who think they're heroes. Drop by www.trcameron.com and take a look!

Until next time, Joys upon joys to you and yours – so may it be.

PS: If you'd like to chat with me, here's the place. I check in daily or more: https://www.facebook.com/ AuthorTRCameron. Often I put up interesting and/or silly content there, as well. For more info on my books, and to join my reader's group, please visit www.trcameron.com.

My father was fond of saying my best trait was also my worst trait. I'm stubborn. Now, my relationship with my father was 'complicated', and that saying was aimed as yet another joke at my expense.

But he was right, sort of.

I have recently gotten a reminder of the value of that saying, and just how much of the wonderfulness that makes up me that he missed.

It started with trying to do some of the things I had put off between moving to Austin, house buying, and then all of 2020. (2020 is probably going to become code word for monumental cluster fuck.)

One item on my list was to get a physical and find a general practitioner. One visit, though, lead to a few tests, which lead to a lot more doctors and before I knew it – a few interesting diagnoses. I'll keep this part short.

Turns out I had an impressive hiatal hernia and an enlarged thyroid – no symptoms. Maybe. It's kind of fun when you see specialists and get to watch their eyes grow when they find out just how far things have failed. Then they would ask me the question again. "Are you sure? No symptoms?"

Nope. Again, well, maybe.

Two things were probably happening. It came on so slowly that I was the frog in a pan of water as it slowly turned hotter. I didn't notice. The other was that I had things to do so I kept going. It wasn't big enough to get me to stop and pay a lot of attention That stubborn trait may have been at play.

Anyway, both were far enough along that it wasn't if they had to be repaired, but when. One surgeon had an opening in two days so I took it. And voila, a week ago the hernia was fixed. A week and a half from now the thyroid will be vanquished and I will be learning to deal with that too.

Here we are at the place where stubbornness is going to come in handy, and where there's more to me, if someone just looked more closely, that is serving me well. After operation number one I tried to get back up and return to semi-normal and for once, it didn't work. Even doing a series of small chores in one day added up to a miserable evening.

It didn't take long for me to notice that if I wanted to get better, I needed to change my behavior. Added plot twist – I live alone with two dogs and things still need to get done.

I could have chosen to hang on to stubborn and get more frustrated or knuckle down and just do it. But instead, I did this wonderful thing that was always just on the other side of stubborn.

I reached out and asked for help from everyone around me. For little things mostly. Take the garbage cans to the street. Walk the dog. Come and sit next to me. The response has been immediate and amazing. I even made it clear that these requests were going to continue for probably the next month.

That second operation is looming and will take an entirely new type of adjusting, but I'll get there, and I'll do it with help.

Once again, I was reminded that most of us want to give as well as receive. We want to be wanted, even in the smallest of ways and I ended up giving myself a gift as well. Closer connections, more rest, and a reminder the helpers are always there when we look for them. (Thank you Mr. Rogers) How weird that from some of the toughest patches of a journey come the sweetest memories. More adventures to follow.

If you enjoyed this book, you may also enjoy the first series from T.R. Cameron, also set in the Oriceran Universe. The Federal Agents of Magic series begins with Magic Ops and it's available now at Amazon and through Kindle Unlimited.

FBI Agent Diana Sheen is an agent with a secret…

…She carries a badge and a troll, along with a little magic.

But her Most Wanted List is going to take a little extra effort.

She'll have to embrace her powers and up her game to take down new threats,

Not to mention deal with the troll that's adopted her.

All signs point to a serious threat lurking just beyond sight, pulling the strings to put the forces of good in harm's way.

Magic or mundane, you break the law, and Diana's gonna find you, tag you and bring you in. Watch out magical baddies, this agent can level the playing field.

It's all in a day's work for the newest Federal Agent of Magic.

Available now at Amazon and through Kindle Unlimited

OTHER SERIES IN THE ORICERAN
UNIVERSE:

THE LEIRA CHRONICLES
SOUL STONE MAGE
THE KACY CHRONICLES
MIDWEST MAGIC CHRONICLES
THE FAIRHAVEN CHRONICLES
I FEAR NO EVIL
THE DANIEL CODEX SERIES
SCHOOL OF NECESSARY MAGIC
SCHOOL OF NECESSARY MAGIC: RAINE CAMPBELL
ALISON BROWNSTONE
FEDERAL AGENTS OF MAGIC
SCIONS OF MAGIC
THE UNBELIEVABLE MR. BROWNSTONE
DWARF BOUNTY HUNTER
CASE FILES OF AN URBAN WITCH

OTHER BOOKS BY JUDITH BERENS

OTHER BOOKS BY MARTHA CARR

JOIN THE ORICERAN UNIVERSE FAN GROUP ON FACEBOOK!

CONNECT WITH THE AUTHORS

TR Cameron Social

Website: www.trcameron.com

Facebook: https://www.
facebook.com/AuthorTRCameron

Martha Carr Social

Website: http://www.marthacarr.com

Facebook: https://www.facebook.com/
groups/MarthaCarrFans/

Michael Anderle Social

Website: http://lmbpn.com

Email List: http://lmbpn.com/email/

Social Media:

https://www.facebook.com/LMBPNPublishing

https://twitter.com/MichaelAnderle

https://www.instagram.com/lmbpn_publishing/

https://www.bookbub.com/authors/michael-anderle